One More Ride

Samantha Montague

This book is a work of fiction. Any references made to historical events, real people, or real places are used fictionally. Any other names, characters, places or events are products of the author's imagination. Any resemblance to actual events, places, or persons living or dead is entirely coincidental.

ISBN-13: 978-1-7369310-9-7

Cover design created using Canva.

This one is for my family.

To Josh, Shelby & Lucy - I love you all beyond measure.

To my readers - I hope you enjoy part two of Ayla and Kane's story. Your support and kind words have been incredible. Thank you for waiting!

Prologue

Tiny white flakes float down as I stare out the window into the yard. My body gives a shiver, even though I'm inside and holding a steaming mug of coffee. I focus on my car, currently parked in Dad's driveway, as I watch the fine white powder start to stick to the surface. Dad's cruiser is gone. He left for the station about an hour ago to start his shift.

We celebrated a quiet Christmas together two days ago, and I've been staying here for the past few days. I always come home and stay here with him through the holiday. This year I needed it even more; the apartment just feels so empty without Cora.

My eyes move away from my car, stopping on the large black truck now parked in the driveway. I couldn't believe it when he showed up here last night. I have Cora to thank for that. A few months ago, I had promised that I'd come to South Carolina to visit for New Year's. She had been disappointed that I hadn't made the trip for Thanksgiving, so when she and Ryder offered me a free trip I couldn't refuse. But I was expecting a plane ticket, not Kane Donovan in my driveway.

I feel him move behind me and it's like he's a magnet drawing me in. It's taking every ounce of strength I have to resist him. I'm going to give him a chance to show me that he's changed, but I'm leaving my guard up. *He hurt me and it's going to take some time…*

Five months earlier...

Chapter One

Ayla

There's a faint buzzing in my ear as I stare at a poster hanging in front of me with giant purple letters asking me if I took my prenatal vitamin today.

"Ayla…Ayla?" The soft voice breaks through my daze and I shake my head, trying to clear my brain. "Are you okay?" the quiet question fills the air as I lift my head to a wide-eyed face.

"I'm sorry. I'm just a little tired," I answer as I take in her concerned look.

"That's understandable, it's actually a symptom of early pregnancy," she offers and I nod softly. "I'm Veronica and I'll be assisting Dr. Jones with your IUD removal procedure today. I just have a consent form for you to read over and sign. Did you have any questions before we get started?" she asks handing me a clipboard and pen.

"No…no. I think I'm all set," I whisper as my eyes run over the sheet of paper. The words swirl into a blur on the page, but I lift the pen and scrawl my name at the bottom of the page before handing it back. She turns, setting the clipboard down on the countertop before moving towards the exam table. I watch as she opens a small drawer at the base and reaches in, revealing a cloth gown.

"I'm going to step out of the room for a minute so that you can get changed. You can leave your top on, but everything from the waist down needs to come off, and the gown should open towards the back," she says with a small smile as she sets it down on the exam table. The door closes behind her and I reach for my waistband, peeling my leggings down and away from my body. I feel like I've lost ten pounds in the past two days. I've been so nervous that I've barely been able to eat anything, my stomach just can't handle it right now.

But food has been the least of my worries. I can't even begin to imagine how Kane is going to take the news. And I've kept my communication with Cora limited to texting. I knew if I actually talked to her, that she'd be able to tell that something was off. Texting over the past couple days has made it much easier to hide. Kane is a completely different story. There was no way I could avoid talking to him for two days, and the second I heard his voice I wanted to tell him…I really did, but I just think it will be better to tell him in person.

I slip my arms through the large holes in the gown and wrap it around my back, loosely tying the long strings together before stepping up and taking a seat on the edge of the exam table. My teeth chew lightly at my bottom lip as I wait. My head is full, spinning with all the possible scenarios that could play out when I tell Kane. My imagination is on overload and I can't take it.

After my positive pregnancy test, my doctor had sent me immediately for an ultrasound. Because of the IUD, she was concerned that the egg might have implanted in my tubes. The wait for her call afterward was only an hour, but it felt like forever.

"The pregnancy is a normal and viable implantation," she had started. "At this point, after seeing the ultrasound, I think it would be safer for both you and the pregnancy to go ahead and remove the IUD. That is, if you plan to move forward with the pregnancy. If not, then I can provide you with some other options," she explained. "Of course, the removal itself does still have some risks to the pregnancy, but they are much lower than leaving the device in place," she had continued once I confirmed that I intended to keep the pregnancy.

After my confirmation, she had also ordered more blood work and set up today's appointment with the OB-GYN for my IUD removal. My fingers twist in my lap as I continue to wait patiently, her words echoing in my mind. Waiting for this appointment has been torture. I've spent all my time hoping that the IUD wouldn't cause something to happen before the removal, but then also having the building anxiety of having it removed and the potential risk that the procedure holds. Plus, there's the challenge of accepting that this is all real and actually happening.

God, I wish Cora was here with me right now. I'm leaving for South Carolina in two days, and I can't wait to see her smiling face again. I really need her right now, and I know that even if Kane rejects the pregnancy, that Cora will have my back and support me no matter what. That's what we do for each other.

But before I take my trip south and have the chance to tell Cora or Kane, there is someone else I have to tell first. I have to tell my dad.

My knees are spread and my feet are settled in the cold metal stirrups. Guys are so lucky they never have to experience this feeling of being completely on display. My eyes find a spot on the ceiling to focus on as I try my best to relax.

"Okay, Ayla. I want you to take a deep breath. You'll probably feel some pressure as I remove the IUD, but it shouldn't be painful," Dr. Jones explains. I immediately feel a slight tug, like someone is pulling at the back of my bellybutton. But as soon as I feel it, it's gone.

"That's it. It's out. You can go ahead and sit back and up if you're ready," she offers happily. I slide my butt back against the table paper, creating a loud crinkling sound through the room.

I meet her gaze as she pulls off her gloves, tossing them in a nearby trashcan before turning towards the small sink. She turns the water on and I watch as she washes her hands, creating a soapy lather and then rinsing. She pulls out a few brown paper towels, patting her hands dry as she turns back in my direction.

"The IUD came out really smoothly and easily. That's definitely a good sign, but you may still have some faint spotting or possibly even light cramping or discomfort. If you start to have any heavier bleeding or overly painful cramping, please call the office right away," she explains and I nod in agreement.

"Also, I would recommend starting a daily prenatal vitamin. And I'd like to see you back here in about a month, as long as you don't have any unexpected symptoms before then. Do you have any questions for me?" she asks as I try to process everything she's telling me.

"Actually, I do have a couple questions," I tell her, remembering the two questions that came to mind over the past couple days.

"Okay," she acknowledges. Her arms cross over her chest and she leans back against the counter, waiting for me to continue.

"So, when this happened, I didn't know. And obviously I thought the IUD was working, so, well…I was drinking. It was bike week and I was out with friends having fun. Should I be worried about the alcohol?" I ask softly.

"Well, generally speaking you're a healthy young woman. Unless women are actively trying and paying extra close attention to their cycles, most women don't know that they're pregnant during those first few weeks. So, you aren't alone with this concern. I get this question from a lot of women. And while I can't give you a definitive answer at this point, I can tell you that there's little chance that the drinking you did had any effect on the pregnancy. From this point going forward you should cut out all alcohol. When was the last time you had a drink?" she asks.

"About a month ago, around when it happened. On a daily basis, I'm not really a big drinker. I tend to let loose when I'm out with my friends or it's a special occasion," I share.

"Okay…okay. Did you have another question?" her eyebrows raise and I'm sure it's because she needs to get moving to her next patient.

"Yes. Is it okay to travel? I'm supposed to leave for South Carolina on Friday. That's where the father is…" I start to offer more than necessary.

"Yes. You are perfectly safe to travel. That usually only becomes an issue towards the end of the pregnancy, when you're closer to the due date. Are you anticipating relocating to be closer to the father?" she asks and her question catches me slightly off guard.

"Um…I'm actually not sure. My best friend lives there now, and I know she'll be supportive, but the relationship with the father is really new. This obviously wasn't planned, and in all honesty, I'm not sure how he's going to react.

I know Dad is home when I hear the cruiser pull in the driveway and the car door slamming closed. My heart is racing by the time he steps inside. I spent most of my day packing, but I knew I needed to see him and tell him before my trip.

"Well…well…well…this is a nice surprise to come home to. My favorite daughter brought me pizza and beer," he smiles brightly.

"Very funny. You do remember that I'm your *only* daughter, right?" I shoot back, knowing that I might not be his favorite anything after tonight. Dad has always tried to be reasonable and understanding, especially since he played both the dad and mom roles as I was growing up, which I know wasn't always easy. But telling him that I'm pregnant; this is a level I'm not sure either of us is ready to deal with.

I watch as he takes a seat at the small kitchen table and unlaces his shoes, pulling them from his feet.

"Ahhhh. That is so much better," he breathes out as he feet flex and stretch. "So, did you just want to have some dinner with your old man tonight, before you leave to see that young man who's waiting for you?" he asks as his eyebrows lift and a grin grows quickly across his face.

"I did, but I actually have something I wanted to talk to you about too," I hesitate slightly.

His eyes roll. "Please don't tell me that you're moving down there like Cora. I mean, it's your life and I know that she's your best friend and that you really like this guy, but that would be a really big step," he tips his head questioning the severity of what I'm about to drop on him.

I pull out a chair and sit beside him at the table, watching as he fills his plate with pizza. My stomach growls, but I know that I won't be able to eat anything until I get my nerves under control.

"I'm not moving, at least not yet," I grin and watch his eyes go wide. "It's…uh…I'm…uh…I'm pregnant," the words finally tumble out. He coughs, almost choking on his pizza and his face turns red as I carefully slide the beer across the table in his direction.

"Obviously this wasn't something I planned for, but I've decided that I'm going to keep it," I tell him. He tips back the can of Bud, taking a large gulp, drinking what I'm sure is at least a third of the can. He sets it back down with a solid clink on the table and his face is unreadable.

"So, what you're really telling me is that I'm going to be a grandpa?" his eyes light up and a small smile forms. I manage to nod in recognition. This is not the response I was expecting. He slides forward on his chair and his arms close tightly around me.

"Sometimes surprises are just what we need. And you know that I'll be here for you, no matter what," his whisper touches my hair and I feel the warm tears pooling on my lower lids as I remember Grandma Rose using the same expression about surprises.

"You just tell me what you need and how I can help, and I'm there. What does Kane think about all of this?" he questions actually using his name this time.

"Well, I haven't told him yet. I know that sounds really bad, but I was thinking it would be better to tell him face-to-face," I explain. "Do you think that's wrong? Should I have told him?" I question suddenly second guessing myself.

"No. No, you're right. Doing it in person will be better. Plus, a day or two isn't really going to make much of a difference in the big scheme of things. What about Cora?" he asks.

"I haven't told her yet either," I confess seeing the look of shock fill his face. Cora and I have shared everything since we were teenagers, and it's been so hard keeping this from her, but I really didn't want to tell her over the phone. "She's picking me up at the airport tomorrow. I'm planning to tell her on the drive from Charlotte to Rock Hill," I explain.

"Well, honey, I can't say that I envy the position you're in right now. This is going to be one heck of a trip, spilling this secret. Doesn't really sound like much of a vacation," he comments. "Do you think you're ready for this?" he asks and I pull in a deep breath.

"No…not really," I confess as I reach into the pizza box and pull out a slice.

Chapter Two

Kane

"Kane!" Drake shouts, breaking through my thoughts as I sit, sipping my coffee in the clubhouse. I'm fucking exhausted. I've been dragging ass, moving around on fumes for the past month. It's strange how one week with Ayla managed to change my entire existence. Sleep has been the worst since getting back from New Hampshire. It didn't take long for me to get used to her curled up beside me and now it just feels like something's missing when I climb into bed at night alone.

Plus, when I do close my eyes, all I can see is the vivid image she left with me last week. She was so fucking sexy, letting me watch her while we were Facetiming. It took her a minute to get into it, but God damn, she gave me a show I'll never fucking forget. Every time I think about it, I get hard again. I don't think I've jerked off this much since

I was fourteen or fifteen, fresh into puberty and swiping my old man's Playboys.

"Kane!" Drake growls louder.

"Yeah, yeah…I fucking heard you, asshole. What the fuck do you want?" I roar back. All the boys know I've been testy for the past month, but this last week I know I've been completely unbearable.

"We just got a call. There's a car broken down on I-77 that needs a tow. The car overheated or some shit. I think it should be a pretty easy call, if you think you can handle it. I'd go, but I'm just about to pull a car in for an oil change," he announces.

"Yeah, I got it," I answer, standing from my chair and tipping back the last of my coffee. "Hey, Prospect, come clean up my shit!" I yell back towards the bar where Timmy, our newest prospect, is busy sweeping the floor.

"No problem. Got it V.P.," he replies as my boots stomp across the floor. I step out the door and start to move across the parking lot, following Drake towards the large garage doors.

It's not long before I'm pulling the truck up in front of a white Honda CR-V parked on the side of the interstate. It's only a couple hundred feet from the exit ramp. It's shit luck that the driver didn't make it off the highway.

I swing my door open and climb carefully from the cab. I move around to the passenger side, attempting to avoid any oncoming traffic as I approach the waiting car. I rap my hand against the window and the driver's side door pops open instantly.

"Careful," I warn as cars continue to speed by. As she steps out and moves around the vehicle, her long honey blonde hair swings with each step. Her face lifts and I feel like I've been punched, all the air leaving my lungs.

"Kane?" she questions, lifting her sunglasses revealing her wide blue eyes. How can she act so surprised? She couldn't have forgotten that I drive the tow truck on occasion, and even if it hadn't been me driving, she could've easily run into me back at the shop. I clear my throat and pull in a deep breath of fresh air.

"Taylor. It's been a long fuckin' time," I breathe out. "Did you forget that I drive the truck sometimes?" I can't stop myself from asking and her face flushes.

"Actually, I didn't call. The battery on my cell is low and I was afraid it was going to die, so I texted my mom and she called for me," she explains.

"Oh…okay. So, any idea what the problem is with the car?" I ask.

"This is a little embarrassing to admit, but I'm pretty sure it's just out of gas," she cringes slightly. "The gauge has been acting funny lately, but I really thought I had enough in the tank to get off the exit and to the gas station," she explains.

"No problem. I've got a gas can in the back of the truck. Let me grab it and we'll see if that's the problem," I offer as I move back towards the truck to retrieve the bright red container. "Go ahead and pop the latch for me," I tell her.

She moves back around the car, reaching down below the dash, and the small door swings open revealing the gas cap. I twist it off and quickly push the nozzle in, tipping the can slightly.

"So, how have you been?" her voice breaks against the sound of the traffic passing.

"Good. I'm good. How about you? I heard you got married and had a kid," I reply casually. It's small, but something changes in her eyes when I mention the kid.

"I did. Actually, it's two kids now. Two little girls, if you can believe it. Three years old and nine months. They're a handful," she laughs softly.

"I bet. So…uh…what are you doing back here? I thought you settled in Texas, close to your sister," I ask remembering the trip I made to confront her when she left.

"I'm still in Texas, but we've had some family stuff going on. My dad got sick, cancer, so I've been trying to make a trip back home every couple months just to help out. I don't want my mom to get too overwhelmed," she explains.

"Shit. I'm sorry. I hadn't heard about your dad. I hope he's okay," I offer, even though the guy was always a complete prick. No one deserves that shit.

"The outcome looks good. His doctors are amazing and they caught it pretty early, so we're really hopeful," she shares. "So, what about you? Wife or kids?" her question hits me full force.

"No," I chuckle. "Someone special though, but it's new. Like brand fucking new, but this time I think it's real," I tell her.

"That's good. You know you deserve to be happy too," she smiles.

"Yeah, I'm just starting to realize that. And Ayla, she's a special one. She's actually flying in tomorrow," I feel my lips curl as my head floods with images of my girl and what I plan to do with her when I can finally touch her again. Taylor's eyebrows pinch and I wonder if I'm sharing too much.

"Where is this *special* girl coming from? Please don't tell me that this is some online match-making website or something," she laughs at me.

"No. Believe me, we've met, in the flesh," I say with a big grin so there's no mistaking my meaning. Taylor's cheeks flush a deep red and her eyes drop to the ground.

"Sorry, just a little fun. I didn't mean to embarrass you. Actually, I met her at a bike rally in New Hampshire that the boys and I went to in June. We've kept in contact since, and believe it or not, her best friend just moved here to shack up with Ryder," I drop a name from her past. Her eyes lift back up to meet mine.

"You didn't embarrass me... I guess I just forgot how open you guys are with all that stuff," she tries to lie. "Wait a minute. Did you just say that Ryder is living with someone?" she questions with shock clear on her face.

"I did. Crazy, right? He fell head over fucking heels, then dragged the poor girl back here with him. There's something about those girls up north. Sexy as hell with attitudes to fuckin' match. We both caved," I chuckle.

"I can't even imagine. Please don't tell me that Fifty has settled too. If you tell me he's married with kids or something, I might just die right here," she lets out a laugh.

"No. I don't think that motherfucker will ever settle down. Fifty loves the ladies too much, or the pussy at least," I tell her.

"Well, please don't hold back. Actually, I guess it's probably true," she shrugs me off.

I pull the nozzle back and twist the gas cap back in place before snapping the small door closed again.

"Why don't you go ahead and give it a try," I tell her.

She slides back into the driver's seat and I hear the engine come to life. I raise my arms up like I just saved the fucking day.

"Ta-da! That should at least get you off the highway and to the first gas station, then you can fill up the tank," I tell her.

"Thank you so much. What do I owe you?" she questions.

"You know what? No charge this time. I'm in a good mood today and I didn't even really have to do anything, other than catch-up with an old friend," I say.

"Really? Thanks, Kane. That's so sweet of you, are you sure?" she asks.

"Positive," I confirm.

"I guess I owe you a favor if you ever need one," she offers with a soft smile.

"No need for favors," I reply with a light double-tap on the roof as she pulls her door closed and I start to walk back towards my truck.

I sit for a second in the cab as she pulls away. My phone buzzes where it's mounted against the dash, and I see Ayla's name light up on the screen.

"Hey, sweetheart," I answer. "Are you all packed and ready for your flight?"

"Actually…" her quiet voice breaks and my chest tightens.

"Actually, what? There is no fucking actually. You better be on that plane tomorrow morning or I'll be coming to get you," I practically growl. I'm hit instantly with her laughter in response.

"I'm just teasing you. Yes, I'm packed and ready and I can't wait to see you," she gushes.

"Damn, baby. Don't do that to me," I reply as I breathe out a sigh of relief and her soft laughter continues. "Shit. Sweetheart, you know I'd gladly stay on the phone with you all damn day if I could, but I'm parked in my rig on the side of the highway. I should probably get moving and get back to the shop. Can I call you back in a couple hours?" I ask.

"Of course. I'll talk to you later," she replies easily.

"I love you, sweetheart," I tell her.

"I love you too," she breathes out, and just hearing her say it makes my heart go wild.

As I tap the screen to end the call, I instantly wonder if I should have mentioned Taylor. This probably wasn't the right time, but I can tell her later or maybe tomorrow. It might be easier to explain if we're face to face and she can see that I have no residual feelings. Fuck, it's been years since I've had to think about shit like this. I put the truck in drive and pull out into the flow of traffic. I really hope I don't fuck this up.

Chapter Three

Ayla

I can't believe we managed to pull it off. After ending my call with Kane it's clear that he has absolutely no idea. Cora and Ryder were waiting for me when my flight landed in Charlotte about an hour ago. I'd probably be with him by now, if we hadn't stopped to grab lunch.

"I'm gonna run to the men's room. Baby, could you get me another beer if the waitress comes back?" Ryder requests softly against Cora's neck. Her cheeks flush and she nods. He stands from the booth and her eyes follow him as he moves across the room. She finally glances back in my direction when he disappears behind the swinging door.

"Girl, you better eat something. You know that Kane's going to keep you up all night. You're going to need your energy," she laughs loudly.

"Oh, shut up," I reply rolling my eyes and tossing a small French fry across the table at her. I ordered food, but the way my stomach is twisting, I've only been able to take a few small bites.

"I, um…I have something I need to tell you," I say as my fingers twist together in my lap under the table. I had really wanted to tell Kane first, but my nerves can't handle much more. Telling Cora will give me a practice run, and hopefully relieve some of the built-up anxiety.

"Okay…what's up?" her eyebrows raise in question.

"I'm pregnant," I blurt out the words and watch her mouth fall open.

"What?! That can't be possible…your IUD. Plus, weren't you and Kane careful? You know that's our deal, we're always supposed to use protection," she glares at me.

"My IUD was defective. And, no, Kane and I weren't careful every time. I know we should have been, but a guilt trip about using condoms is not what I need right now. I really just need my best friend," I admit.

"Well, shit…" she breathes out.

I reach for a French fry and shove it in my mouth, suddenly feeling famished now that I'm not holding the secret in. I pick up my sandwich to take a bite, but then the questions start.

"So, you're keeping it? Do you know how far along you are? How are you going to tell him?" they pour out one after the other.

"Do you think we could talk about this later, you know, when we're alone? I really don't want Ryder to know before I tell Kane. Can you please just keep this between us, at least until tomorrow?" I beg. Unfortunately, I was so focused on Cora that I completely missed

Ryder headed back towards the table. His large frame slides back down beside Cora and he plants a kiss to her temple.

"Impossible. My girl doesn't keep secrets," he grins. "Now, what the fuck are you trying to hide?" he questions roughly. My body stiffens slightly as I search for the right words.

"I'm not trying to hide anything. There's just something I want Kane to know before the rest of the club finds out," I tell him and his eyes grow wide. I don't know how he did it, but I can tell just from the look on his face that he's figured it out, without me even saying anything.

"Holy shit. You're pregnant, aren't you? Damn, baby girl. Kane is going to flip the fuck out. I hope you're ready to deal with the fallout," Ryder offers, not holding anything back.

"Believe me, I know how Kane can be. I've dealt with his mood swings before, but it's different now…he's different now," I remind him. "Plus, he can't be mad at me. It's not like I did this alone. He definitely played a role."

"Yeah, yeah, I get that. He should have wrapped his shit up, that was stupid on his part. But, sweetheart, I've known him a long time and I can almost guarantee that his first instinct is going to be that you somehow did this on purpose," he gives me his opinion.

"I hope you're fucking kidding. Is that seriously what you think? Is that what *you* would think if it was you?" Cora's face turns red and I can see her anger starting to bubble.

"No, baby. I'm just saying how I think Kane is going to react," he explains as his arm moves up behind her, trying to pull her in close. She flashes a grin and wiggles away playfully.

"I hate to break it to you, but you aren't going to sweet talk your way out of this one," she says.

"I bet I can make it up to you later," he coos softly as his lips drop to her neck.

"Okay, you two. No one wants or needs to see you going at it during their lunch hour. Do you think you can reign it in until you get home?" I laugh lightly as I remind them that we're in a family restaurant.

"Maybe they don't need to see it, but I bet some of 'em would want to," Ryder adds with a smirk and I feel my eyes roll.

I pick up my glass of water and take a long drink as I process Ryder's response to my news. Maybe that's how Kane would have reacted when I first met him, but he really is different now, *right?* I know he loves me...he'll have to see that I'm completely surprised by this situation too, *won't he?*

The last leg of the drive is short and sweet. As we drive through the town, my eyes are drawn to all the beautiful old buildings. I know this is just a small part of Rock Hill, and I hope I get a chance to explore a little while I'm here.

Ryder pulls the truck into a large flat parking lot situated between two buildings. He parks beside one of them and I feel my heart pounding heavy against my chest when I see the line of bikes. The bright sunlight hitting the metal and chrome creates an almost blinding glare. My eyes move to the door and I find the Lucifer's Savages MC symbol painted on the outside of the building. It matches the symbol stitched into the back of their leather cuts.

"Welcome to the clubhouse," Ryder turns back with a broad smile.

"It's Friday, so if you're lucky he might still be inside finishing up his lunch hour. If not, then he'll be over at the garage," he offers, pointing across the lot to another oversized building with three large garage doors.

I open my door and hop from the backseat of the truck, following Ryder and Cora's lead as they move towards the clubhouse door. It opens and I'm instantly met with music and laughter. There's no doubt…he's definitely here. There's no mistaking that deep rough laugh that pulls at my core. My heart thumps rapidly against my chest, just knowing I'm about to see him again.

I let my eyes move around the room and I'm actually surprised at what I see. It's gorgeous. I expected a dive, something dark and dirty. But the place is large and open, and it's filled with beautifully carved wood pieces making it feel warm and inviting. My breath catches and I stop in my tracks when my eyes fall on Kane.

He's sitting just a couple feet away with a few of the guys, just as Ryder had predicted. His back is to me and he has a black cap sitting backwards on his head with the word SAVAGE in bright white letters. I watch as Ryder and Cora keep moving until they both pull out chairs and sit down, easily falling in with the group.

"About time you showed your fuckin' face around here. What happened? Your girl moves in and you don't come to work anymore?" Kane questions with a rough laugh.

"You don't even want to fucking start that shit with me. I was doing you a favor not being here," Ryder responds as his eyes lift in my direction, hiding the secret that Kane still doesn't realize. I can't see his face, but I watch his body react. His shoulders square off and his back tightens, pulling at the fabric of his shirt.

I inch closer, holding my breath in hopes that he won't turn around. I've come this far; I want to pull this surprise off and see his reaction. I'm close…close enough to touch him. My hands move quickly as I cover his eyes and drop my lips to his ear.

"Guess who?" I say, unable to keep my smile from growing.

"Ayla! No fucking way!" his surprised words hit the air and he's out of the chair in a fraction of a second. His arms move around me and he lifts me from the floor as the excitement takes over.

"How?" he questions.

"Surprise," I offer softly as his lips finally cover mine and the rest of the room swirls, disappearing around us.

"You're fucking welcome," Ryder's voice breaks through and the room fills with laughter as Kane starts to move across the floor. I lift my legs and curl them around his torso as his large hands move to cup my ass and give a little lift.

"We're not gonna see those two for the rest of the night," I hear another voice followed by more laughter.

Kane stops abruptly and breaks our connection. One hand moves to his jeans and he fishes a set of keys from his pocket. His arm lifts slightly before letting them fly across the room and towards the table, which is now behind me.

"I'm done for the day. Someone else is on tow truck duty," he smirks and a deep pulse runs through me. We're about to be alone for the first time in weeks and I know Kane is going to spend the rest of the day working on me.

Chapter Four

Kane

The feeling of her warm thighs wrapped around my body is even better than I remember. I can't believe she did this. This is the first time, in a long time, that I've been genuinely surprised by someone.

"God damn, sweetheart. I can't believe you're actually here," my ragged words slip out between us. My head drops to her silky brown hair and I inhale deeply. My cock throbs and instantly goes rigid as her sweet scent fills my nose.

I cover her lips again as I step through the doorway and into the bedroom I keep here at the clubhouse. I kick the door closed with my boots, letting it close with a heavy thud. I move across the room and lower our bodies together to the waiting bed. She tastes like fucking heaven as my tongue continues to move over hers and she moans softly against my mouth.

As I break from her and pull back, my breathing is ragged and out of control. I can't believe she's here and in my bed. I need her now. Honestly, I need her more than I've ever needed anyone or anything in my entire existence.

"Clothes off, baby," I force out in short breaths. "If this first time is quick, I promise I'll make up for it later," I grin knowing that I'm bound to explode the second I'm inside her. Her plump pink lips form a perfect 'O' as she processes my words, and I know I'll need to feel them later too.

Reaching back, I grip my t-shirt and pull it up over my head in one swift motion. I drop it to the floor and move my attention to my jeans. I manage to kick off my boots as I fumble with the fucking zipper that doesn't want to budge. I hear her soft giggle and look up to the bed, finding her gorgeous body on display. Her leggings and shirt are already gone, leaving only the thin lace of her bra and panties covering her smooth skin.

Her smile sets me on fire and I quickly move back to my zipper, needing to get these jeans off faster than my fingers will move. She laughs again, obviously finding my struggle amusing. It finally budges and I breathe out my relief as I shove them down and off my legs.

I look back to the bed and her blue eyes pierce into mine as her fingers move to the front clasp on her bra. I watch her make the smallest twisting motion and it pops open, and she spills out perfectly. I lick my lips as she pushes the fabric down her arms and away from her body. She knows just how to get me worked up even more.

I take a step forward, and reach my hands out, grabbing her ankles. Giving an easy pull, she slides down the bed and a slight look of surprise touches her lips making her somehow sexier. I lower myself until I'm hovering over her, the heat pulses between our bodies still not touching. I bring my head down to her chest, finally bringing my lips and tongue to touch her skin for the first time in weeks. She's so fucking sweet and I instantly crave more.

I make a slow circle with my tongue, watching as small goosebumps rise on her skin before I cover her nipple completely and pull her in deep. Her back arches underneath me and she breathes out a soft moan, prompting me to suck harder. She touches my shoulder lightly before raking her fingers down over my biceps and gripping my flexed muscles.

I release her, letting her pop softly from my mouth as I shift my focus. My fingertips begin to travel over her heated skin until I reach her waistband. I curl them under the edge and peel the fabric down off her legs and away from her body. I toss them and she giggles. My cock already throbbing, twitches at the sound and the burn radiates deep into my belly. I lower my eyes to meet hers and grip her knees, pushing them apart and stepping forward to take my rightful place.

I drop one hand letting my thumb find her sensitive clit as my fingers slip easily against her wet heat. She bucks lightly as I move against her. As much as I want to feel her come on my fingers, my dick is screaming at me and this time I need to be selfish.

"Are you ready for me, sweetheart?" I ask already knowing just how fucking ready she is. "You're so wet, baby. This is going to feel so fucking good," I praise her as I continue to work her slick pussy.

"Please, Kane," she pleads. And hearing her breathy voice whisper my name and begging for me to make her feel good is more than I can take.

My fingers move, wrapping around my hardened shaft as I press my throbbing cock to her soaking wet entrance. I hold my breath and bite my lip to keep from coming just at the contact. Rubbing against her, I let the wetness coat the tip before plunging deep and feeling her along every inch. Her pink lips make a small 'o' and her cheeks flush a soft shade of pink as I pump into her

"Fuuuck…your pussy feels amazing," I growl and almost immediately her soft walls clench, somehow squeezing me even tighter.

"Oh…my…God," her short breaths hit my ears and I know she's there. Thank Christ, because there is no way I can hold on any longer. A hot wave runs through my core and I let go.

"Fuck…gaaahhh," a roar tears out from deep in my chest as I spill into her.

Ayla's head rests against my chest, her tight curvy body is curled up right where it belongs. My arms pull her in tighter when I feel her shiver against me, the thin sheet covering our bodies is offering little warmth. I should pull up a thicker blanket, but I can't bring myself to move away from her, even if it's only a few feet.

I had intended to spend our first night back together at my place, but her surprise definitely killed that plan. And now that she's naked in my bed, here at the clubhouse, there is no way I'm asking her to put clothes back on. One taste definitely wasn't enough, and I fully intend to fuck her until we both pass out from exhaustion.

Plus, I know what a fucking hassle it will be if we try to leave right now. It's Friday night and I'm in no mood to deal with the scene that I'm sure is raging down the hallway. Her fingers run softly up over my abs and chest, breaking into my thoughts.

"Everything okay?" I question when she wiggles beside me.

"Mm-hmm," she breathes out as her fingers continue to trace over the black ink covering my skin. "I just can't believe that I finally made it here. I was so afraid that Cora or Ryder would spill the secret and the surprise would be ruined," she tells me and I can hear the mixture of relief and happiness filling her words.

I pull her closer, letting my palm slide down the side of her body as I explore her curves. A small giggle bubbles up, escaping past her lips, and I know I've hit a magic spot. I pull my hand back up and do it again and she breaks into full blown laughter. My lips curl into a smile as I let the sound fill me.

My hand finally settles on the curve of her ass and I hear the change in her breathing. Her reaction tells me that she's ready for round two just as much as I am. I bring my other arm around to get a grip on her.

"Come here," I breathe out heavily as I lift her up and onto my body.

I can already feel the heat pulsing between her thighs as she straddles my torso. The sheet falls down and away from her body and my dick hardens at the sight of her generous tits bouncing softly as her body shifts and she settles into place. My hands lift to hold the weight of her chest and my excitement grows when I see her nipples harden under my touch.

"Bring these right here," I request as I release her and tap my finger lightly against my lips.

Her eyes widen and her face flushes as she slowly leans into me. I lift, bringing my mouth to meet her as I once again pull her deep into my mouth. She moans softly and I feel her warm wetness spread over my hardness as she begins to rub against me.

God damn. My girl needs to be fucked and I am more than happy to give her just what she wants. I release her from my mouth and watch in awe as she continues to work her body over mine. Her eyes are closed and her face is lifted toward the ceiling, and she looks like she could come at any second. She is so fucking sexy.

My hands move to her hips, lifting her and her eyes pop open. She quickly realizes what I'm doing, and she holds herself up just long enough for me to move. As soon as I'm in the right spot, she drops.

"Holy shit!" I can't contain myself as she starts to ride me. She is fucking perfection and I'm completely mesmerized as enjoy everything about this moment.

"Yes…yes…" she cries out. I knew she was almost there, but damn; my girl was ready. I grip her hips and lift, thrusting deep into her and giving her exactly what she's begging for. Her warmth spreads over me as she tightens and her body begins to tremble.

"That's it, baby," I encourage as I watch her come apart. I pull her down again, letting my cock fill her completely as I let a deep cleansing roar roll off my chest, claiming her once more as mine.

Chapter Five

Ayla

I collapse against Kane's sweat covered chest. My own chest heaving as I try to catch my breath. I'm not sure what just came over me. I couldn't stop and the way he felt inside me was indescribable. I was so wet and horny; it was almost embarrassing. I mean, he gets me excited every time, but this was different. It was all consuming, like I couldn't get him fast enough or deep enough. It has to be something hormonal…the pregnancy. How am I going to tell him?

His thickness gives a slight twitch as I shift to slide off of him. I relax back into the crook of his arm, resting my head against his chest. I melt into the warmth of his body and inhale deeply, breathing in his strong scent. Just being in his presence again has completely overwhelmed me and I can't seem to get a grip. It's hard to believe that this undeniably sexy man is really mine.

"That was..." he breathes out heavily, still recovering from me practically mauling him. "Shit, sweetheart. Every time with you has been like a fuckin' dream, but that...that took it to a whole new level," he grins in obvious enjoyment. His fingers make a smooth trail up my arm and my body shivers at the gentle contact.

"I missed you," I whisper against his chest as I curl in deeper.

"Sweetheart, you have no idea how much I missed you," his voice drops low against my ear and I know he means every word.

I love him. This amazing man makes me feel alive in a way I never have before. But it's not just the sex and the excitement he creates, it's the moments like this. The way he holds me and the quiet whispers. I feel safe when I'm wrapped in his arms.

I feel my eyes start to close, finally giving in to the building exhaustion. Yet another annoying side effect of the pregnancy. The day of travel and excitement, not to mention the mind-blowing sex we just had, has completely worn me out. I try to keep my eyes open, but it's no use. The heat from Kane's body is pulling me under and I'm not strong enough to fight it right now.

A loud thumping wakes me and my eyes open at the sound. Kane is still beside me in the dark room. It's hard to tell what time it is without any windows. I let my eyes adjust briefly to the darkness before reaching my hand over and tapping the screen on my phone to check the time. It lights up brightly, blinding me for a second, and the time flashes, revealing 6:12 a.m. Jesus, I must have been tired. I can't believe I slept straight through the night.

The thumping grows louder and becomes steady, then the moaning starts. Oh my God, really? And then it dawns on me, if I can hear them, could they hear us last night? Should I care? I guess I should be glad it's just moaning, with some of these guys, I'm sure I could hear a lot worse coming through these walls. As I lay back down against my pillow, Kane rolls to his back and his eyes fly open.

"It is way too early for this shit," he groans before his eyes move over me and a broad grin spreads across his face. "Well, God damn…I think I spoke too soon," his eyes darken as they rake over me, and he lets a low chuckle slip past his lips. And my body shivers knowing that he could make me moan like that in about ten seconds if he really wanted to.

"Do I even want to know who that is?" I question softly. He shakes his head and lifts his fist to the wall behind the headboard.

"Shut the fuck up!" he growls as his fist pounds against the wood, but the moaning continues without pause or regret. "I can't believe you're really here. For a minute I thought maybe I was dreaming," his eyes soften as he turns his attention back to me.

"It's definitely not a dream," I say lifting to my elbow and bringing my lips to his. His thick arms curl around me, settling comfortably around my lower back. His lips break from mine and he rests his head back against the pillow.

"I gotta say, I could really get used to waking up with you in my bed," he smirks.

"And is that because you love me, or because you think you're going to get some?" I smile back watching his eyebrows lift. He slides one hand down and away from my lower back, taking a firm grip on my bare ass cheek.

"Oh, I know I'm going to get some," his cocky answer creates a deep pulse straight through my center as my desire pools quickly between my thighs. His palm moves in a slow circle over my skin before he offers another strong squeeze. "We both know I'm right," his voice turns to a husky whisper and I shiver just knowing what's about to happen.

I step back into the hallway after taking a few minutes to freshen up in the bathroom. After our early morning of fun, tangled up together in the sheets, both Kane and I fell back asleep. It was just after nine when we finally crawled out of bed. Kane suggested getting some breakfast before he finally takes me to see his real place.

He gave me a big explanation about the room at the clubhouse, as if I didn't know what it was really for. I got the *"I just keep it so I can crash after parties"* story. But I'm not stupid, I know these guys all have rooms so they have a place to bring their endless string of girls, or the girls they want to fuck on the side. And knowing that he's had other girls in that room makes my stomach turn, especially when I think about how many there have probably been over the years. But the bigger question that's taking root is, after years of living this life, will he be able to stay faithful?

I swallow hard as I think of the tiny seed growing deep in my belly. I think I'll try to tell him at breakfast. After last night and this morning, he should be in a good enough mood to handle the news.

My booties click lightly against the hardwood floor as I move down the hallway to meet Kane in the main bar area. I step into the open space and I easily find him standing larger than life, leaning casually against an open doorframe across the room. As I move towards him, his eyes rake over me unapologetically and his lips curl into a wide smile.

My breath catches and I feel my cheeks flush. I lift to my toes when I reach him, kissing him deeply and not giving a shit about who might be watching.

As we break, my eyes catch on a small group of lounging females. It's too early for them to be here to hang out. Based on their somewhat ragged appearance, my best guess is that they're stragglers from the party last night. One with shoulder length blonde hair seems to be glaring at me, and I notice one of the other girls touch her arm causing her to finally turn away.

"Girls, retract those fucking claws. It's too early for that shit," Army's voice booms as he walks up behind me. "You should really be more welcoming to our guest. This is Ayla," he introduces me. "And she's going to be spending a lot of time here with us, so I suggest you all remember exactly who this clubhouse belongs to. If you want to keep hanging out then you need to cool it with the fucking daggers you're all throwing. She was invited here and none of the Savages are going to tolerate your shit when it comes to her," he warns. I finally let out a breath, feeling relieved that it wasn't just my overactive imagination. But I also can't help but wonder why Kane let Army do the dirty work.

"We were all wondering when you were going to show up. Kane's been such a bore since he got back from Laconia," the blonde turns, flashing me a smile that instantly makes me want to vomit. There's no doubt in my mind now, he definitely did something with her at some point in time. Maybe even all of them, as they all sneer and giggle at my expense. My eyes drop to the floor and I feel Kane's body stiffen beside me. His finger touches my chin, lifting my face until my eyes meet his.

"Ignore them, sweetheart. Remember what I told you. All that was my life before. I can't hide it; you know how I've lived. But I'm with you now…just you," his words burn into me and I nod in response. "C'mon, let's go get some food," he adds.

"Give me a minute. I want to look around a little, you didn't give me a chance to actually see this place when I got here yesterday," I manage a small smile. There's a beautiful dark wood bar with plenty of stools and even more seating at scattered tables and chairs. I step closer, letting my hand run over the surface of the bar. "This is beautiful," I observe and I'm met with laughter.

"Fuckin' A., Kane. I think your girl really likes the hard wood," Drake chuckles.

"Another word and you're fuckin' dead," Kane growls as I turn to see his vibrating body. The whole room seems to go quiet and his dark eyes move back to me. "Go ahead, sweetheart. Take a look around and ignore this asshole," he says.

Aside from the bar, I find the other half of the room set up with a couple pool tables and an area for playing darts. The seating surrounding the gaming area is all softer couches and chairs. I move closer, letting my hand move over the black felt covering the pool table, I find the Savage's symbol etched into the fabric.

"You should see your boy play, he's pretty fuckin' good," Army steps up beside me. But as I lift my gaze, my eyes are drawn to two large black sliding barn doors that I hadn't noticed yesterday. I'm not quite sure how I missed them before, they're definitely a focal point. I step towards the one closest to me and bring my hand up to touch the smooth black finish.

"Sorry, darlin', but that one is off limits. Only Savages are allowed in church," Mickey appears beside me. "But feel free to check out the other room," he offers with a soft chuckle. I keep walking to the left and lift my arm to slide the next door open, but Kane's hand is on mine before I can manage to move it.

"Nope," his voice is soft against my ear. "What is it with all you motherfuckers this morning?" he growls loudly to the rest of the room.

"Hey! I was being nice," Army reminds him.

"Fine, guess what? Army, you get to come to breakfast with us, my treat. The rest of you can fuck off," he grins.

"Wait. Why can't I go in this room?" I ask.

"Shit. It's not that you can't, I just... Shit, sweetheart, it's not really a room you're going to want to think about. I feel my eyebrows lift with curiosity. Now I need to know.

"Tell me. Now," I demand as my hands settle on my hips. His eyes go wide and he chuckles at my stance, but he's not getting off the hook that easy. His large hand moves back to the door and he pushes it, easily sliding it open on the frame.

"Don't say I didn't warn you," he tells me, taking a step back so I can finally look into the room.

It only takes a second for me to realize why he tried to stop me. It's clearly a room meant for sex. My eyes move over the couches and chairs filling the room. Everything is black and gray, making the room seem dark and intimidating. I take a hesitant step forward with my heart wedged tightly in my throat. My fingers pull at the knob on a small drawer, and when it slides open it's fully stocked with assorted boxes of condoms. I quickly slam it closed as my stomach turns.

I have no illusions. I know what this brotherhood includes, but the idea of Kane in this room makes me want to vomit. My chest burns and I realize I've been holding my breath since my feet stepped through the door. I inhale deeply, trying to pull myself together. I turn quickly, needing to get out of this room fast. I walk straight past Kane's large looming frame without even a glance. I can feel everyone watching me and I just need to get away.

I keep walking, straight across the room and pull out a stool at the bar. When my eyes lift, I'm met with a fresh-faced kid who can't be much older than eighteen or nineteen. The patch on his chest reads PROSPECT, but I don't recognize him from bike week.

"You're not Billy," my voice is barely a whisper.

"No, ma'am. I'm Tim. You…uh…you don't look so good. How about I get you a glass of water?" his blue eyes soften and I nod in response.

Behind me, I hear the sound of the door rolling closed, then heavy boots moving across the floor. I know it's only a matter of seconds before Kane is at my side again. He moves in behind me, placing his hands flat on the bar, caging me in as his warm body presses into my back.

"I tried to tell you," his deep voice fills my ear. "But remember, I'm not that guy anymore." I can't speak or offer any type of response.

"Too bad…not everyone can handle the fuck room. But it's a lot of fun," the acid voice burns into me and I already know who it is. It's the blonde, the one who was glaring at me a few minutes earlier. This is her way of confirming what I already knew. She's been with Kane…in that room. My mind is spinning and I push out a deep breath.

"Fuck room? *Seriously?* You guys actually call it that? Not very creative," my thoughts are a whisper as they hit the air.

Kane's body shifts to turn, taking a wide defensive stance. But before he can say anything, Fifty's voice echoes through the room.

"Brittney, would you shut the fuck up and get your nasty ass out of here. No one wants to hear your shit. Just go," he fumes. I don't have to turn to look. I hear the clicking of heels on the floor and I know that she's leaving with her group of friends.

Fifty steps in behind the bar, taking the glass of ice water out of Tim's hand and setting it in front of me.

"Drink up," he says giving me a small wink.

"Thank you," I mouth and he nods. I take a deep breath and lift the glass to my lips, letting the water cool me. Kane's soft lips brush my temple.

"I'm sorry about that. Do you still want to get some breakfast?" he asks. I nod and lift my eyes back to Fifty.

"You're coming too. I owe you a meal after that," I tell him. He leans down, resting his elbows on the bar.

"Don't even think twice about those petty bitches, they're not worth it. They're fucking miserable when they're hungover," Fifty whispers for my ears only. "And just so you know, a few of us are actually pretty original. We call it the dark room," he offers with a soft chuckle.

"Hey, asshole. Unless you want me to rip your fuckin' throat out, I suggest you get your mouth away from my girl's ear," Kane growls and his body tenses beside me. I finally look, touching his arm lightly.

"I'm okay. Let's just go eat," I manage a small smile as I slip from the stool. I slide my hand into his, trying to convince him that I'm fine, but as we walk towards the door, I can feel the heaviness in the pit of my stomach dragging me down with each step.

Chapter Six

Kane

God fucking dammit.

I knew. I knew the second I walked out and saw Brittney that this was going to go south fast. She's a regular who's been hanging around for a few years. From the minute she stepped foot in the clubhouse she had her eye on me, and she wasn't fucking shy about it. But I wasn't interested. I mean, she's got the look and she knows how to play the fucking game, but it was almost too easy. I've always been one who liked a little more of a challenge. Well, maybe not always. I guess I liked the easy ones too, but I just wasn't interested in her. Unfortunately, my continued rejections only made her more persistent.

A couple months before our trip to New Hampshire, the boys put together a huge blowout for my twenty-fifth, and I got so fuckin' lit I couldn't see straight. I had been messing around all night with this chick, Dani. She's another regular who knew what I liked. But when we made our way into the dark room, Britt tagged along and both girls were into it. Of course, I went along for the ride. It was my birthday and I wasn't going to turn down two for the price of one.

The memory floods my mind and I feel sick. I try to push it away as I ride with Ayla clinging to me, finally on the back of my bike again. I know I have no real reason to feel guilty for the shit I did before I even knew her, but I can't seem to stop the gnawing feeling that's settled deep in my gut. I need to get my fuckin' head straight.

I park my bike alongside Fifty and Army. Ayla slips easily from the back, quickly pulling off her helmet and handing it to me. Her eyes linger on my face and her hand lifts, her thumb gently rubbing the scruff on my jawline.

"I'm okay. I'm stronger than you think," she says, obviously sensing my mood. I push out a deep breath. Ayla is finally here with me and I'm not going to let some distant fucking memories ruin what we have between us.

"Okay. Let's go get my girl some breakfast," I wrap my arm around her as we move towards the door.

I just inhaled a tall stack of blueberry pancakes along with a plate of scrambled eggs and a double side order of bacon, and Ayla has barely taken three bites of her French toast. Between watching her pick at her plate and Fifty eye fucking the waitress, I am more than ready to leave. I know she told me that she was fine, but she's obviously still letting the interaction with Brittney bother her. I need to get her back to my place so we can talk without an audience. The last thing I need is Fifty and Army listening to every word I say.

"Well, it's Saturday night, kids. Will you be partying with us tonight, or are you having your own private event?" Army's eyebrows lift in question. He knows after that show this morning there's no way I'm bringing Ayla back to the clubhouse tonight. Britt is sure to be there with all the other regulars, and I'm not going to deal with any more of that shit.

"No. We'll be staying at my place for the night," I offer a clipped answer.

"That's probably the safe bet, brother. But you're gonna miss one hell of a party," he says grinning back.

Ayla continues to stare at her plate, pushing her fork around without actually eating anything and not joining in the conversation. I can't take any more. I lean into her and she springs up in surprise.

"What's going on in that pretty little head?" I whisper against her ear as I watch Fifty hand the waitress a wad of cash. Ayla shakes her head.

"I think I'm still just a little tired from traveling yesterday," she tries, but I can tell it's something else.

"Okay," I mutter. I'll let it go for now, but we will be having a conversation once we're alone.

After a quick ride across town, we're finally at my place. I keep her hand in mine as we climb the front steps, only letting it go so I can unlock the door. I hold it open and let her step inside as I follow close behind her.

"Well, this is it," I offer with a small wave of my arm. It's not much, but it's mine.

She turns back and smiles at me and I see some color has finally returned to her cheeks. I shut the door behind me and move to close the distance between us. I wrap my arms around her and drop my lips to her ear.

"You know I love you, right? I need to know that you believe me when I say that all that shit is in my past. My club is my family, and I love my brothers, but you are the only woman I want," my voice is low and full of need as I say the words. My cock jerks in my jeans feeling her warm body pressed into mine.

"I know. And I trust you," she breathes out softly and it's all I need to hear. I lift her easily, and her legs wrap around me as my mouth covers hers. She melts against me, soft and sweet, the taste of maple syrup lingering on her lips. As I carry her towards my bedroom, I let it all go. She's here and she's mine and none of that other shit matters right now.

Chapter Seven

Ayla

Once again, my hormones are in complete control. Kane's tongue twisting with mine sends a deep stimulating pulse straight to my center. I can feel the warm wetness growing as he carries me through the house. He sets me down lightly, breaking our connection and the hunger in his eyes consumes me.

"Take 'em off," he growls, gesturing to my clothes. "All of them," he adds and my body clenches at the thought.

I begin to peel the layers away from my body. Even in my rush to get them off, I can't take my eyes off him as he does the same. The black ink flowing over his hardened muscular frame has me panting with anticipation. I know exactly what he's capable of, and I'm completely ready for him.

My breath catches as my fingers start to pull at my panties, and I find them already soaked through. Kane's eyes move to mine and he steps forward. I feel the warmth radiating from his body as he closes the distance between us and his hand lifts to my chin.

"Is everything okay?" he questions, having heard my reaction.

"Yeah, I was just a little surprised," I offer without going into detail.

"By what?" confusion takes over his face and I feel my own grow warm under his watchful gaze.

"It's my panties. They're…they're…" the words catch on my tongue as his hand leaves my face and moves between my legs.

"God damn, sweetheart. You are so fucking wet. And, baby, that is such a fucking turn on," he lowers his voice and his eyes darken as he strips the fabric quickly from my legs and I step out of them. He drops them to the floor and I watch as he starts to pull off his boxer briefs, carefully releasing his hardened length. My center pulses seeing it rigid and ready for me. I can't wait to feel him inside me again.

His eyes flash when he catches me staring and I know we're both feeling it. His lips drop to touch my neck, creating a soft trail down to my collar bone before moving down to my chest and pulling me softly into his mouth. His tongue swipes at my nipple and I can't stop the soft moan from escaping through my parted lips. He releases me at the sound and my body shivers as the cool air kisses my warm wet skin.

"I want you on the bed, now," he demands and this time I shiver with excitement.

I comply, letting my body fall softly against the bed. But before I can get too comfortable, his large hands are on my hips. He grips my waist and flips me easily with a quick twisting motion. His strength is unmatched. I lay on my belly and his hands move to curl around my ankles. He drags me gently to the edge of the bed and I can't stop the giggle of delight that falls out. The anticipation is more than I can take.

"Now lift that ass for me, sweetheart," his deep words have me dripping with anticipation.

I scoot back and lift for him, and his fingers move to meet my waiting heat. He begins to play, spreading the pooling wetness. Sliding forward, he rubs my sensitive clit and I'm panting as I buck against him, craving more and he lets out a soft chuckle. His hand disappears and I feel his strong, pulsing cock take its place at my waiting entrance. He rubs against me softly and my pussy aches, my body begging for Kane to fuck me again.

"Remember our first time?" his husky voice questions.

"Yes…" I force out my answer through ragged breath as I struggle with my building anticipation.

"Then you know what I want to hear," he replies deeply. And I know. He already knows how much I want him right now, but he wants to hear me say it. It turns him on even more to have me begging for it.

"Please, Kane. I want your cock…I need you to fuck me," I beg. He plunges deep and I cry out as the pleasure hits full force.

"That's right, baby. I'll fucking give it to you, just the way you like," he growls as he slams into me and my body accepts each thrust willingly.

With my head resting against Kane's chest, I let the familiar warmth of this moment run through me. This man is all I want, and the realization hits me that it's finally time. I've been so caught up in reconnecting with him that I've already let too much time go by. I have to tell him about the baby.

I lift slightly and rest my chin on his chest, finding his eyes closed. He looks completely relaxed and content. I push out a soft breath, trying to find my courage.

"Kane," his name comes out barely above a whisper.

"Hmmm," he breathes out.

"There's something I need to tell you," I start as his eyelids pop open and his eyebrows pinch in question.

"What is it, sweetheart? You know you can tell me anything," his voice is soft and it gives me a glimmer of hope. I bite my lip and swallow hard, trying to find the right words.

"I know. I'm just a little nervous," I admit truthfully.

"Well, now you're going to have to tell me something, because I can't imagine why you would ever be afraid to tell me anything," he replies taking a harder tone.

I push out a deep breath and let my head fall back down on his chest. My finger moves over his skin, tracing the black ink. He clears his throat and I know that it's my warning that his patience is running thin.

"I'm pregnant..." I finally breathe out the words and my teeth clamp down on my bottom lip.

His body tenses beside me and he immediately shifts, lifting off the bed in one quick movement. His bare frame paces beside the bed and I watch his skin tighten as his back and shoulders flex. He's too quiet.

His eyes burn dark when he finally stops moving and looks back at me. It reminds me of when he flew into a rage and beat up a random drunk guy who decided to grab my ass during bike week. It's unnerving and almost scary.

"Are you fucking kidding me right now?" the words tear from his chest as his body vibrates. Okay…not really the reaction I had hoped for. "Did you do this on purpose?" he questions roughly.

I feel my eyes widen in shock. Ryder's words from yesterday suddenly echo in my brain. He can't be serious. What could I possibly have to gain from doing this? As I lift to sit, I pull the blanket up around my chest, suddenly feeling completely exposed.

"Are *you* kidding me right now?" I throw his own question back. "Why would you ever think I did this on purpose?"

"Girls do shit like this all the time to try and trap guys like me…guys who don't want to settle down," he responds roughly, running his hand up through his hair. I can't help but let out a rough laugh in response. Is he actually serious right now?

"I think maybe you've seen one too many movies. And I'm so sorry to disrupt your carefree lifestyle, but you do realize that this wasn't exactly in my plans either. I'm supposed to be going back to school in the fall. At least it's nice to know what you really think of me," I push out as my own anger begins to simmer.

"Maybe you thought a baby would lead to something else. Marriage or some happy homemaker shit like that. Sorry to break it to you, sweetheart, but that's not gonna happen with me," he replies, reminding me of the Kane I first met at bike week.

"I can't even believe you right now. I'm not trying to trap you. You do remember that I was actually engaged when you met me, right? And I ended that, so I could really give a shit about getting married right now. This was an accident. My birth control was defective," I try to explain, but I can tell just from his stance that he's not going to listen.

"How long have you known?" he growls out the question.

"A week. I had no idea, but they did some tests and told me during my doctor's appointment," I answer.

"You've known for a week? A fucking week and you didn't think maybe you should tell me?" he roars.

"I wanted to tell you in person. Obviously, this whole trip was a huge mistake. Give me a minute to get dressed and I'll call Cora to come pick me up," I offer pulling myself from the bed.

"Fuck that. Actually, fuck this. I'm leaving. I need to get some fresh air," he says reaching to the floor for his boxer briefs. He pulls them quickly up his legs before grabbing his jeans. I understand the initial shock of it, but he is being so stubborn and mean. It hurts to hear him say these things.

"You don't even want to consider my side of this?" I question in pure disbelief. I really believed him when he claimed to love me. I guess maybe it really was nothing more than just sex to him. He just let himself get caught up and told me things he didn't really mean.

I watch as he continues to pull on his clothes, slipping into his boots and pulling a t-shirt down over his head before finally sliding his arms into his leather cut. He's really going to leave me here. He turns and walks out the bedroom door without another word or even a glance back in my direction.

"You're an asshole!" I scream at the top of my lungs as the anger and hurt run through me.

The door slams and only seconds later I hear the roar of his bike as he speeds away. My body collapses back to the bed…the bed he just ruined me on. He took my body, loving me so deeply and then only minutes later he broke my heart. I'll never forget the hatred in his eyes as he accused me of plotting this. I let the sobs take over as my body shakes uncontrollably and the tears flow in a steady stream.

Chapter Eight

Kane

My blood is boiling. I'm on fucking fire as I ride into the wind. I lean heavy on the throttle, letting my bike take me away as fast as fucking possible.

I can't fucking believe this shit. I actually fell for the *"I'm on birth control"* story and let my guard down. I've never fucked without protection, but I completely fell for Ayla's charms and her sexy little body clouded my judgement. Fuck. Even when I was an idiot teenager, young and fucking horny as hell, I always wrapped my shit. My dad always warned me…

God dammit.

Girls have tried to convince me before, but I never caved. But Ayla was different. She had me wrapped around her little finger and I fucking fell for it.

I hit the highway and completely let go. I ride fast, needing to get away from my own thoughts. I keep riding until the sun sets in the distance and the darkness grows around me. In all honesty, I'm not even sure how far I've gone, but my hands and legs are starting to ache.

I slow and pull off the next exit, stopping at the first gas station I come to. I pull in under the canopy and top off the tank before making my way inside. I hover in front of the beer coolers, waiting for some college age douches to grab their Saturday night six pack. They shuffle away quickly when they look back and find my looming presence. They seem to sense my mood, and tonight is not a night to fuck with me.

I step up and glance through the glass but as I look, I realize that none of this weak ass beer is even going to come close to taking the edge off. I need something stronger. I yank the door open and grab an energy drink instead. Stomping over to the counter, I hand the cashier enough to cover my drink and gas, then I step back outside into the warm summer night air.

I pull into the parking lot at the clubhouse and it's fucking jammed. This might be a fucking mistake, but I can't go home yet. As I walk into the raging party, I know I'm going to get a few looks and questions, but I intend to grab a bottle from behind the bar and head straight back to my room. I'm not in the mood to talk to anyone or take any shit. I just need a place to be alone.

It's loud and hot as fucking hell as I weave through the hazy cloud of smoke, my eyes fixed on the bar ahead. Timmy, our newest prospect since patching in Billy, is manning the bar tonight. Poor S.O.B. gets to watch all the shit go down, but doesn't get to join in the fun yet.

"Hey V.P.," he grins when I approach.

"Hi, kid. I need a bottle of Jack," I tell him.

"Sure, no problem," he says, quickly setting the black label on the bar in front of me. My palm wraps around the glass and as I turn to move, I realize I've been spotted.

Fuck.

Army sidles up beside me with a big fuckin' grin. He's already three sheets. "Hey, V.P., didn't expect to see your ass here tonight. Thought you'd be occupied all weekend," he chuckles before turning his attention to Timmy.

"Prospect, get me five shots of Fireball and three of Jager," he tells the kid before looking back in my direction. "Where's the queen hiding? What does she think of this crew on our home turf? It's a little different than bike week," he grins.

"She's not here," I growl before twisting open the bottle and tipping it back, taking a long slug.

"That was quick. What the fuck did you do?" he accuses.

"I didn't do shit. Maybe she did something," I suggest.

"I fucking doubt it. That girl is about as close to perfect as they come," he grins having no fucking clue what he's talking about. Just as I'm about to rip into him, Timmy saves his ass. He slides a tray up on the bar, holding the shots Army's waiting for.

"Take your shots and get the fuck out of my face," I snarl.

"Yes, sir," he shoots back as he picks up the tray and moves across the room towards a table full of waiting females.

I lift my bottle again, tipping it back and letting the amber liquid burn its way down. As I pull it away from my lips, Brittney's blond head turns and her eyes twinkle at me from her seat at the table. She tips back a shot and then stands, moving in my direction.

She's dressed to party, in typical Saturday night fashion. Her long legs are covered in fishnets, and a pair of short black shorts with knee high boots. Her chest is barely covered in a black crop top that looks more like a bra than a shirt. These girls dress to fuckin' kill. Her cherry red lips curve into a smile as she steps up in front of me.

"Hey," her voice is barely audible over the loud music.

"Hi, Britt," I offer a clipped response as I take another small sip from the bottle clutched in my hand.

"I just...I wanted to say that I'm sorry for earlier. I never meant to cause a scene or any trouble between you and your girl," she starts and I know this is complete bullshit. That's exactly what she meant to do. She wanted Ayla to know that she had been with me. Earlier I was completely pissed, but between the fight with Ayla and the Jack seeping into my veins, I really don't give a shit at the moment. "If she's here, I'd really like to introduce myself and say sorry," she adds.

"Well, she's not here," I mutter.

"Oh..." she breathes and her hand lifts to my chest, her red nails matching her lips. "Maybe you should come sit with us," she points to the area she came from and I shrug in response.

Fuck it.

I stomp across the room and drop my body into an oversized leather chair, keeping my bottle pressed tight against my knee. After watching Army bring back the third round of shots since I sat down, the numbing effect from the Jack has finally started to kick in. My eyes start to glaze over, but a roar of excitement catches my attention, pulling me from my whiskey fueled haze.

I look up to see Brittney and one of the other girls in full lip lock, giving anyone watching a free show. When they break, her eyes seem to focus on me. I offer a smile and a nod of approval before lifting my bottle again. She reaches across the table and takes a small joint from Mickey's outstretched hand, as he grins and tips back a shot of his own. She pinches it between her fingers and brings it slowly to her lips, taking a long drag, as she stands and starts moving in my direction.

She stops in front of my chair and leans down, letting the smoke go in my face and I breathe it in. I take it from her hand and bring it to my lips, pulling a deep drag into my lungs and letting it seep in. Her hands touch my knees as she drops her mouth to my ear.

"Lexi and I are going in the other room to get a little more comfortable. We thought maybe you might want to join us…or at least watch," she coos. I push the smoke out through my lips and nostrils, and lift my heavy eyelids.

"Sounds like fun," I nod.

As I stand from my chair a large hand grips my shoulder and I look back to find Fifty. Bastard has the worst fucking timing. I don't need his shit right now.

"What are you doing, brother? Where's Ayla?" his question creates a fire inside me. I don't want to hear her name right now.

"None of your fucking business, *brother*," I snarl in response.

"Maybe you should go back to your bunk and sleep this shit off. I'm not falling for whatever this sorry ass act is that you're putting on.

You and I both know that you're about to screw up the best thing that's ever happened to you," he says.

"Well, I don't remember asking your fucking opinion," I reply. "I don't know why you even bother picking up the pieces every time I fuck up? You think I don't know that you want her? You've been fucking drooling over Ayla since we met her. Here's your fucking chance. Why don't you go save her this time, instead of worrying about me?"

"Don't you dare say shit like that to me. And when you wake up from this tomorrow, I hope you remember that I tried to stop this shit from going down. You're a selfish motherfucker and you're going to lose her just because you can't handle the fact that you might actually care about someone other than yourself. I really thought you were past all this," he seethes.

"Well, I guess I'm not. Now get the fuck out of my way. I've got a show to watch," I say as I move across the room and disappear behind the waiting black door.

Chapter Nine

Ayla

All night long I kept trying to close my eyes, but there was no way I could sleep. After I scraped myself up and got dressed, I moved to the couch. Staying in that bed was impossible. I don't know how many times I checked my phone during the night only to find nothing. I almost called Cora, but I couldn't bring myself to face the reality yet. I kept hoping that he would cool off and come home. I knew he was upset, but I honestly can't believe he left me here all night and never even called or texted.

There's only one place I know to look for him. I roll from the couch and grab my phone off the small side table. I quickly arrange an Uber and grab my bag, deciding to wait outside.

Stepping into the clubhouse, I'm hit hard with the lingering stench. This place reeks of smoke and stale beer, and whatever else they were doing in here last night. A few hungover gazes meet mine, but they're all quiet as I inch through the room. I slip into the darkened hallway, heading straight for his room. My heart pounds against my chest as I reach the door, afraid of what I might find on the other side.

I take a deep breath and turn the knob. I don't even bother knocking, I'm not giving him a chance to hide anything. Shit. It's empty and his bed is still put together. If he's not here, *where is he?*

I turn to leave and I hear another door open behind me. I glance over my shoulder to find Fifty's towering frame. He pulls a dark t-shirt down over his tattooed torso and then runs his hand up over his face and hair. His eyes go wide when they stop on me.

"Where is he?" I ask simply and he starts to shrug, but I can already tell he knows something. "And don't even think about lying for him. I just need to know…" my words hang for a second and he shakes his head. I can already feel the small pools gathering on my lower lids and my bottom lip begins to tremble.

"He was pretty fucked up last night, sweetheart. You might not want to find him right now," he tries to warn me off but it's not going to work. I told Kane that I wasn't going to be one of those girls who would look the other way. I made it perfectly clear that if he wanted me to be his, then I was going to be the only one.

"Please, just tell me," I try to appear strong, but my voice betrays me as my words shake.

"He disappeared into the dark room last I saw. I'm sorry, sweetheart," his head drops and his hand runs over the back of his neck.

I turn back around without another word. As I step back into the large room, all eyes seem to move to me. They all know. I move towards the large black door, still closed from the party last night. My palm touches the wood and I push. It slides silently along the track, and despite the number of people who I know are watching, I think I could hear a pin drop.

My eyes move around the room, finding small clusters of half-naked bodies, still sprawled across various pieces of furniture. He's not hard to find. His large frame sits propped up, with his head back and his eyes closed. His t-shirt and cut still cling to his body, but my eyes fall to the mess of blonde hair resting in his lap.

My hands drop to my knees and a cold shiver runs over my skin as the breath leaves my body. I manage to push the vomit down and pull in a new fresh breath, filling my burning lungs. My teeth bite hard against my lip as the anger begins to quickly replace the repulsion.

I stand and turn, moving across the room towards the bar. I can feel everyone watching me, but I really don't care anymore. Let them watch. I swipe a heavy white coffee mug from behind the bar and move back towards the open doorway.

"Ayla," I hear Fifty's voice behind me.

"Don't," I warn, letting my eyes burn into him for daring to speak to me right now. I lift my arm and let the mug fly. It hits the brick wall just to the left of Kane's head and shatters loudly before falling in tiny pieces to the floor.

His eyes fly open and his body jumps. The noise seems to wake up most of the room, including the blonde in his lap. A new wave of nausea hits full force when she sits up and I realize that it's the same girl from yesterday, the one he had obviously been with before. And she's topless, on full display. My stomach rolls at the sight.

His wide eyes land on me and he stands. There are so many words on the tip of my tongue as I stand here staring at him in disbelief, but I just can't make any of them come out.

"Ayla, I'm..." his voice is still thick with whatever he put in his system last night. My hand lifts to stop him before he can get any further. I've seen enough.

"Save it. I don't want to hear your bullshit. You make me fucking sick," I turn and move towards the door in a daze.

The sun blinds me as I step outside into the fresh air. I need to get away from this place before he tries to follow me. I let my feet hit the pavement and I start to run. I turn the corner and don't look back. I keep running until my lungs burn and my feet ache.

I finally slow to a walk, trying to catch my breath when I notice people in the distance. I can tell that I'm closer to town, but I'm not sure which direction I was running in, or how far I've gone. I rest my hands on my knees as I pull in a deep breath, but now the sobs kick in and I can't seem to stop.

My phone rings in my back pocket and I manage to slide it out in time to see Cora's name light up the screen. I answer in full blown sobs, no words at all.

"Ay...I need to know where you are," her voice takes a sharp tone. "Fifty called Ryder. Tell me where you are and I'll come get you."

"I...I can't. I need some time alone," I manage to push out through my tears before hitting the end call button. She's my best friend and I know she wants to help, but she's with Ryder now and if I tell her where I am, I take the chance that Kane might find out where I am too. And I can't handle him finding me right now. I just need a little time. I turn my phone to silent and slide it back into my pocket as I slowly pull myself together.

As I walk the tears continue to flow freely down my cheeks. I lose track of time and I can't be sure how long I've been moving when I see the familiar golden arches. I'm not hungry, but I need a place to sit down and get my bearings while I decide what to do next.

The air-conditioned air tingles against my sweaty skin as I step through the door. I look around, and thankfully it's quiet inside. I find a small table in the corner and pull my phone out before dropping into a chair. I see multiple missed calls and texts from both Cora and Kane, but I can't deal with either of them right now. My throat is dry and burning, but I let my breathing start to settle before standing again and moving towards the counter.

"Hi, how can I help you?" a young girl with steaks of pink running through her hair asks.

"Umm," my voice wobbles. "I'll take a small Coke," I say pulling a couple crumpled bills from my pocket and handing them to her. Only seconds later she's handing me the ice-cold cup and a straw.

"Are you okay?" her question is soft and I feel my walls caving.

"No, not really," I answer honestly as I rip the paper off my straw and drive it down through the plastic lid. "I'm from out of town and I got a little lost walking around. Could you tell me what street this is?" I ask.

"You're on Herlong Ave.," she smiles.

"Thanks," I reply as I take my cup back to sit at the same table. I bring my lips to the straw and take a long drink. I'm glancing at my phone, debating whether or not to call Cora to have her come get me, when I see a message from a number I don't recognize. I tap the screen and find that it's from Fifty.

**Hey – It's Fifty. Cora gave me your number. Tell me where you are and I promise I'll come alone.*

I swallow hard and feel a fresh round of hot tears begin to stream silently down over my cheeks. I let my fingers move over the screen as I type a reply.

**McDonalds on Herlong*

I finish what's left of my Coke and stand. I head towards the ladies' room, dropping my empty cup in the trash on the way. Stepping inside the small bathroom, my eyes instantly lock on my ragged reflection in the mirror. I ignore it, and move to an open stall. I use the toilet and as I pull the paper back, I'm met with a bright red stain. In my panic I wipe again only to see more.

I can't breathe. I roll some toilet paper around my hand and shove a wad into my panties as I quickly pull my bottoms back up. I quickly wash my hands at the sink. I need to get back out to the dining room and ask the clerk where I can find the closest emergency room or urgent care center. I step through the door and I see the dark leather. Fifty turns, locking me in his gaze.

"Ayla, darlin', come here," he opens his arms and I move forward, falling against him. My sobs are loud and uncontrollable as he holds my shaking body.

"I need…I need to go to the hospital," my words are muffled against his chest. He pulls back slightly and looks down at me.

"Why?" he questions.

"Something's wrong. I'm bleeding," I explain through the tears.

"Bleeding?" he asks, the confusion clear in his voice.

"I'm pregnant, but now I'm bleeding. Something's wrong," I share and his face goes pale in response.

"That's why Kane was so out of it last night," the realization hits him and I nod. "C'mon," he offers me his arm and leads me out the door towards a large silver truck.

Chapter Ten

Kane

The hot water runs down over me as I try to wash away the unforgivable shit I did last night. I didn't even chase after her; I couldn't. Not in the state I was in. I'll never forget the way she looked at me. She looked at me like I was a stranger, someone she never knew and didn't want to know. And I can't fucking blame her.

She tells me she carrying my baby and my first instinct is to think that she plotted that shit. Then I ran, I fucking ran away without even listening to her. I got so wrecked and ended up… Christ, I can't even think about it. I feel fucking sick. I don't deserve her, I guess maybe I never really did.

Even after showering and sticking my head in the toilet, I still feel like complete and utter shit. I destroyed the one good chance I had. What the fuck is wrong with me?

I feel lost as I sit on the edge of my bed, a towel still wrapped tightly around my waist, my head hanging heavy in my hands. My room still smells of her and the memories from yesterday flood my mind as I sit here. Feeling her body against mine, and then my anger and rage taking over when she surprised me with the pregnancy. I can't believe I left her. I just left her here alone.

My phone makes a pinging noise breaking me from my daze and I stand to grab it off the dresser. I know it's not her, but I can still hope. As the screen wakes up, I see a message from my sister, Leia. As I read over her message, I remember that I told her I'd bring Ayla for dinner to meet her and the kids.

Shit.

**I'm hoping to have dinner ready by 6:30 – but you can bring her over any time. I can't wait to meet her!*

My fingers hit the screen as I type back, **I fucked up. Don't think we're gonna make it.*

It instantly rings in my palm and Leia's name flashes on the screen.

"Yeah," I answer roughly.

"What'd you do?" she questions.

"Just believe me when I say that I fucked up beyond repair. She's fucking gone," my voice breaks letting my weakness show.

"But she just got here this morning, how can she possibly be gone already?" she asks.

"No, she surprised me. She flew in yesterday and it was fucking incredible. Then I acted like an asshole and she left. I'm sure she's with

Cora and I know she's not coming back to me," I admit.

"Well, she knew what she was getting into. How bad of an ass could you have been?" she laughs out the question obviously not taking me seriously.

"Leia, she's pregnant. She told me last night, and let's just say that I didn't react well to the news," I give her a small piece of the story.

"Oh, shit. Wait! Kane, you're going to be a dad," she breathes out.

"She's not going to want me anywhere near that baby. I can't get into it now, but she fucking hates me," I tell her.

"I doubt that she hates you, but you need to fucking grow up a little," she says and suddenly there's pounding on my door. What the fuck?

"Kane!" Cora screams from outside. Oh shit.

"Leia, I'm gonna have to call you back. I've got company and this isn't going to be good," I tell her.

"No problem. Let me know if you need anything, little brother. You may have fucked up, but I'm still your sister and I love ya," she says and I hit end, setting my phone down before moving down the hallway and towards the front door. I pull it open and Cora's voice instantly bombards my senses as she and Ryder step inside.

"I can't believe you. What is wrong with you? You make me fucking sick. How could you? Ayla is my best friend and she loves you. She told you about the baby and that's what you do? You fucked that nasty trash just hours after you had Ayla in your bed. Seriously, what the fuck is wrong with you??" she rants.

I stiffen and swallow hard. I may be a piece of shit, but I'm not going to let her attack me for things I didn't do.

"Hey, I can take a lot of shit. Fuck, I probably deserve most of what you're saying, but I did not fuck Brittney last night. I watched some shit and I know I crossed the line, but I didn't have sex with her," I tell her.

"As if that makes it any better. She won't even talk to me or answer my calls. She thinks you'll find out where she is. But apparently you don't even care, because you're here, at home, taking a fucking shower," she observes.

"Baby, I know you're angry and worried about Ayla, but just try to relax a little. I promise we'll find her," Ryder move his arms around Cora's tiny shaking body.

"Wait. What do you mean, *find* her?" I ask in confusion.

"Well, asshole. When she ran out of the club this morning no one bothered to follow her. And no one has seen or heard from her since, not even her dad," Cora's words create a new feeling of dread in the pit of my stomach.

"You called her dad?" I question suddenly feeling the severity of the situation. "Give me a minute. I've gotta put some clothes on, then I'll go out looking," I say spinning around and heading towards my bedroom as my mind begins to torture me with possibilities.

It's been hours since Ryder and Cora knocked on my door, and still not a single fucking word. We've all gathered back at the clubhouse, trying to figure out what to do next. I can't fucking take this. Cora's phone vibrates on the table and she pounces on it.

"It's Fifty," she breathes as her eyes remain focused on the screen. "He has her. They're at Piedmont Medical Center. It's not good. I need to get there now," her voice is barely a whisper.

"How the fuck did Fifty end up with her? And why is she at the hospital?" I roar. "What did the message say? Read it to me, word for fucking word," I demand.

"Kane, you need to chill the fuck out," Ryder meets me toe to toe. He takes Cora's phone from her shaking hands and gives it to me to read the message for myself.

**Found her. We're at Piedmont Medical Center. They're running some tests but it doesn't look good. She really needs you.*

I hand Cora back her phone. The glassiness in her eyes creates a fresh wave of guilt. It's not Cora's fault, it's mine…all fucking mine.

"I'm sorry," I bite my tongue and apologize.

"C'mon, baby. I'll drive you," Ryder starts to move her towards the door. My boots hit the floor loudly, each step echoing as I follow behind him. But he stops and turns back, looking at me over his shoulder. "Maybe you should just stay here. It might not be the best time, brother."

"I'm going. This is my fault and I need to make sure she's okay, even if she won't talk to me. I just need to know. Don't even fucking try to stop me," my voice is steady but inside I feel fucking defeated.

Chapter Eleven

Ayla

The doctor's words echo in my ears. It's crazy how fast I got attached to the idea of the tiny little seed growing in my belly. It's only been a week, but now that it's gone, I just feel empty. I know it wasn't really in the plans, but the second I found out it was there it became a permanent part of me.

Fifty is here with me. He was here when the doctor gave me the news, saying that one word that caused me to crumble…miscarriage. He's been a rock the whole time, but I finally caved and asked him to text Cora for me. I need her now more than anyone.

There shouldn't be any complications, but the doctor wanted me to say for a couple hours so they could give me fluids. Running around in the heat this morning wasn't the best idea.

"Thank you for staying with me," I sniffle as Fifty stands from his chair when Cora appears wide-eyed at the door. He leans down close to my ear.

"I'm here anytime you need me, darlin'," he offers before placing a gentle kiss to my forehead. God, why couldn't it have been him? Why couldn't I have fallen for Fifty? Why did it have to be Kane?

"Ryder's out in the parking lot. He…uh…he might need a hand with Kane," Cora whispers to Fifty as he approaches the door, but I hear every word.

He can't be here.

I can't see him.

I don't want to see him.

I watch Fifty disappear in a rush and Cora inches forward, slowly taking a seat in the empty chair beside my bed.

"I'm so sorry," she whispers as tears flow down her cheeks.

"Don't apologize. You didn't do anything. I'm sorry I couldn't talk to you earlier, but I needed a minute to get my head straight," I tell her as I feel my own tears start to roll.

"But Kane…the baby…" she can't get her words out.

"The baby's gone," I choke out a sob and she leans forward to wrap her arms around me.

"I need to see her! You have to let me in there, it's my fucking baby!" Kane's deep voice roars through the emergency room.

"I'm sorry, but she doesn't want you in the room. And if you don't settle down, we'll have to call the police to come escort you off the property," I hear a calm but commanding voice reply.

"Are you fucking joking? After all the shit we do for this place. All the charity rides and volunteer work and you're going to pull this shit," Kane's response is anything but settled.

"Kane…" I hear Fifty's voice join the mix and I'm sure he's going to tell him. There is no baby, so there's no reason for him to even be here. A loud crash of clanking metal fills my ears and I know Kane has either kicked or thrown something.

"Get him out of here, now!" the voice of authority returns and only seconds later it's quiet again as the doctors and nurses begin to buzz around as though everything is normal.

"So, do you feel like telling me what happened?" Cora asks softly.

Through a lot of tears and a matched amount of anger, I manage to rehash all the events of last night and my day today. She doesn't interrupt, she just holds my hand and listens as I fall apart.

"I talked to my dad a little while ago. He's going to call the airline for me and arrange a flight home. I'm leaving tomorrow," I tell her.

"But…but you just got here," her lip trembles.

"You know I can't stay. I promise I'll come back to visit when the time is right, but right now I have to leave. Do you think I can come home with you and Ryder for the night?" I ask.

"Of course," she offers a soft smile. Ryder pokes his head through the door and I wonder how long he was standing there without either of us noticing.

"Hey there, baby girl. I'm fucking sorry. I tried to keep him contained, but you know how he can be," he offers before moving his focus to Cora. "I need to get him outta here before he blows up again. I'll have Fifty hang around in case you need anything before I get back. Just call or text me if anything changes," he says and she stands to meet him.

"Ayla's going to stay with us tonight, then she's flying back home tomorrow. I love you," she whispers lifting to her toes and pressing her lips to his. It's so easy to see that they really do love each other.

After leaving the hospital, showering and changing, I finally start to feel a little like myself again. I touch my hand to the soft blanket, letting it run over the surface of the guest bed. My eyes move over the endless stream of texts Kane has bombarded me with.

**I'm sorry*
**Talk to me*
**Please…*
**We need to talk about this*
**Just let me explain*

There are so many, it actually hurts to look at them. I stop scrolling, I can't read them all. I decide to send one simple reply and be done. My fingers move as I type back, **You have to stop. There's nothing more to say.* My thumb hovers for a fraction of a second before hitting send. I set it to silent and drop it on the bed.

There's a light tap on the door and Cora's head peeks in. "Can I come in?" she asks softly. I nod and wave her in, lightly patting the bed so she'll sit beside me.

"How are you feeling?" she questions.

"Dazed, like this is all a bad dream. And honestly, I am so fucking confused. I feel sad, but at the same time it's like, why? I never planned to be pregnant, so I should be relieved, right? Then I feel guilty for thinking that too. And Kane…he just keeps texting and that is making it even harder. I just feel so stupid for believing that he changed. I thought that I would be enough," my voice breaks and I can feel the familiar glaze forming over the surface of my eyes.

"You're not stupid. Please don't ever say that. He did change, really, we all saw it. I think the baby thing just really freaked him out. And he fucked up. He fucked up bad," she offers.

I nod my head in agreement, but my voice gives out and I can't speak. I lift my hands to cover my face as the tears start again for the millionth time since yesterday.

"Hey, I'm sorry," Cora whispers. "How about some food, are you hungry? Or do you want a drink? Ryder can mix a mean cocktail," she offers with a soft laugh.

"No, I'm good. I really just want to curl up and sleep," I tell her.

"Okay, but you know where I am if you need anything," she stands flashing me a small smile before disappearing back through the door.

I lie back and slip my body under the blanket, pulling it tight around me. I close my eyes and let the darkness take over. Right now, I just want to forget.

Chapter Twelve

Kane

I've tried to get her to talk to me. I gave her the night. I can't take this waiting around shit anymore; I have to go see her.

My fist pounds against Ryder's door. I know she's here. She has to give me the chance to explain. I know I was a fucking asshole and I know it looked really bad when she found me yesterday morning, but she needs to know that it wasn't what she thinks.

I lift my fist to hit the door again, but it swings open before I can make contact. Ryder's dark scowl glares at me.

"Kane, what the fuck? I do have neighbors here. You're lucky no one's called the cops with all the fucking noise you're making," he growls taking a casual sip of his coffee.

"Where is she?" I question roughly. I don't have time for a bullshit lecture. "Where's Ayla?" I clarify as if he didn't already know.

"She's gone," his words are clear and simple and I feel my body grow cold as they hit my ears.

"Don't fucking lie. You're seriously going to stand there and tell me she's gone. You're my brother," I start to argue.

"I'm not lying. She really is gone. She caught an early morning flight. Cora took her to the airport a couple hours ago," he shares and my face drops. "Come on in and I'll get you some coffee," he offers, opening the door wider.

I step through and find a seat in the kitchen. Ryder hands me a steaming cup of coffee and I bring it to my lips, blowing across the top. "She really left?" I can't help but question. And he offers a small nod in response as he drags the chair out to sit beside me.

"So, are you gonna tell me what the fuck happened Saturday night?" he questions roughly before lifting his mug again.

"Fuck, man, I don't even know where to start," I run my hand up over my face. "I just fucking flipped. She told me about the baby and I lost my shit completely. I actually asked her if she did it on purpose," I say acknowledging my own stupidity but he nods his head as if he understands. "Then I just left. I left her alone at my place. I went to the clubhouse thinking I could hide out in my bunk, but I took a bottle from the bar and let myself get pulled into the party. I woke up in the fuck room when she threw a coffee cup at my head," I tell him.

"No shit. She really threw a cup at you?" he questions with a grin.

"Yup. It hit the brick wall and shattered right beside me," I answer.

"What were you thinking? Why'd you go in the fuck room? Did you actually screw the girl she found you with?" he asks not realizing who I was with.

"No. Shit, it's all such a fuckin' blur, but no, I can honestly say I didn't fuck her," I tell him.

"But you did other shit?" he questions knowing me too well.

"Fuck. Yeah…yeah, I did. It was Brittney, you know, the blonde who's always hanging around," I start.

"Shit, Kane. That chick is fuckin' crazy and she's had you in her sights for a while. Going in that room with her was real fucking dangerous," he says stating the obvious.

"I know, I know. She had a friend and I just went in to watch, I wasn't going to do shit. But Army or Mickey…shit, one of the guys snagged her friend away and then it was just me and her. She crawled in my lap and used my hand to get herself off," I feel sick as the words leave my mouth. My elbows rest on my knees and I drop my head, taking deep breathes, hoping the nausea will pass quickly.

"That's bad, but it's not the end of the world. We both know it could've been a lot fuckin' worse," Ryder remarks and I know he's right.

"She's never going to forgive me. I wasn't there when she needed me. And the baby… She was alone and now it's gone. I promised her that she'd be the only one and I went and fucked it all up," I exhale.

The front door opens and both our heads lift in that direction. Small, stomping footsteps approach and there's no doubt Cora is home and she's going to rip me a new asshole.

"No…no…no!! I can't even look at you right now. You need to

get the fuck out of this house," she reams into me right off the bat. Ryder stands, immediately trying to settle her tiny vibrating body.

"Baby, calm down," he approaches her softly. "Kane just told me everything, and he didn't have sex with that girl. I know it looked bad, but it wasn't what Ayla thought it was," he tries.

"Don't feed me that shit and try to cover for him. Ayla told me that that girl was completely naked and asleep with her head in his lap. I'm not stupid," she glares at him.

"No one is calling you stupid. I'm just saying he didn't have sex with her. He may have, you know, played around a little, but that's it," he shares flicking his fingers in the air and her eyes turn into dark narrow slits as her face scrunches in anger.

"And, what? You think that's okay? Like you can just go and finger fuck whoever you want and it's no big deal?" she turns in a huff and stomps down the hallway.

Shit. Now I'm getting Ryder's situation all fucked up too. I stand, leaving my still full coffee mug sitting on the table.

"It's okay, brother. You don't need to defend me. I made my own fuckin' bed. Go fix it with Cora. Tell her I'm a fuckin' pig and all that shit," I land a generous slap on his shoulder as I move towards the door.

"You know I'm here if you need anything. And keep your phone on, I might call a meeting later. We have a couple out of state runs we need to figure out. I'll be in touch," he turns to club business.

"Sounds good, brother," I reply as I step outside.

Ryder did end up calling a meeting. It was quick and easy. He needed a few volunteers to make a run to Arizona to pick up some inventory. Normally it would be my scene, but my head just isn't in the game right now and I don't want to be a fucking liability if something shady goes down. Shark, O.B., and Big E. volunteered to make the ride. And they're bringing Billy along for his first real ride since getting patched in.

I tried to hide out in my room after the meeting, but it's the same as my bedroom at home. It's too fresh, it still holds her smell and I just can't take it. I pull up a stool at the bar instead and Fifty takes a seat beside me.

"Are you gonna go after her?" he questions.

"I can't," I shrug him off. I fucked up royally and she's going to believe what she wants to believe. And who the fuck could blame her? She found me passed out with a naked chick in my lap. Not really the easiest situation to try to explain.

"You know, you were a real asshole to me that night," Fifty adds.

"I'm sure I was," I admit even though I don't even really remember talking to him that night.

"Yeah, you accused me of wanting Ayla. Pretty much told me that I could go take her if I wanted to. You were beyond fucked up," he offers what I'm sure is only a small glimpse of what I actually said to him. "Let's just get this shit straight right now. I know that girl is special, but I don't see her like that. I look after her because she feels like my little sister, and honestly, I see you with her and I know you love her even if you can't man up and accept it."

"Hey, Prospect," I holler, getting Timmy's attention. "Give me a bottle of Jack and two glasses," I demand.

"Coming right up," he complies, quickly sliding them in front of me.

I twist off the top and pour the smooth amber liquid, filling both glasses halfway. I push one towards Fifty.

"Sorry, brother," I apologize as I lift my glass and tip it back. "Thank you for being there for her when she needed it."

Chapter Thirteen

Ayla

My phone vibrates, rattling against my side table like it's my morning alarm. I reach my arm out to grab it and finally open my eyes to look at the screen. It's nine thirty already. I had woken up when Dad left for his shift around six, but I guess I fell back asleep.

When Dad picked me up at the airport, he told me that I was coming home with him. I knew better than to argue and, in all honesty, I didn't want to go back to the apartment alone anyway. I see Cora's name, so I slide my thumb across the screen to answer.

"Hi," I greet her with sleep still clinging to my voice.

"Oh, shit. Were you still sleeping? I can call back later," she stutters sounding slightly frazzled.

"It's okay. I should get up and stop feeling sorry for myself anyway. What's up?" I ask. I hear her take a deep breath through the receiver, and something feels wrong.

"It's Kane," she finally says and my stomach twists into a knot. "He crashed his truck last night driving home from the clubhouse." I feel my heart wedge tightly in my throat.

"Is he…is he okay?" my voice shakes and I can feel my eyes glazing over.

"Yes. He got really lucky. He has a concussion and a couple broken ribs; he'll heal. But his injuries are the least of his problems right now," she starts. "His blood alcohol was more than twice the legal limit. Timmy and a few of the guys tried to stop him, but he just wouldn't listen. Ay, he's going to lose his license, and he might go to jail," she tells me. I inhale deeply as my heart dislodges from my throat. I feel like I can finally breathe again now that I know he's alive and okay.

"I'm glad he's okay and that no one else got hurt," I manage to squeak out.

"I know it's all still really fresh, but would you consider talking to him?" her question is soft against my ear and I know she won't push it, but she had to ask because she cares about Ryder and his club.

"I can't. I know he's hurting, but he made his choices. I just…I have to try and let him go. If I talk to him, it will just hurt even more," I tell her.

"And I completely get that, but I feel like you left before you got the whole story. He knows he messed up, but I believed him when he told me and Ryder that he didn't have sex with that girl. I saw it in his eyes," she offers.

"Even if he didn't, he still touched her, Cora. There's no way he can deny that. You weren't there to see it. She was naked and passed out in his lap. Are you going to tell me you'd be okay if you found Ryder in that situation?" I question and from her lack of response I'm sure she turning red just thinking about it.

"Okay…you're right. I know it's not fair of me to even ask," she gives.

"But he's really okay?" I ask again needing confirmation.

"Yeah. He's a little busted up, but like I said before, he got really lucky," she tells me again.

"Will you keep me in the loop when you find out what's going to happen to him?" I ask.

"Of course," she replies softly. We talk for another minute before I hit the end button and our call is over. But I'm sure I'll be hearing from her again soon.

I know talking to Kane right now would completely wreck me, but I decide to reach out with a text. I open my messages and type, **I just heard about the accident. I'm glad you're okay.*

I hit send, not elaborating or attempting to give him any hope. I just want him to know. I watch the three small dots appear and I know he's typing a response, but then they disappear and my heart sinks. They reappear quickly, and my phone vibrates against my palm, revealing one simple word.

**Thanks*

Chapter Fourteen

Kane

"Mr. Donovan," the judge's raspy voice echoes through the quiet room, as he squints at me over the top of his wire-rimmed glasses. "It's been a few years, but I understand that this isn't the first time you've been in this courtroom," he adds.

I offer a small nod and the piercing pain in my ribs takes my breath away. After two days, they finally released me from the hospital. The doctors told me that it could take a month or two for the ribs to heal completely. But now I'm here, at the courthouse, ready to accept my punishment like a man.

"I hope that you realize just how lucky you are. Your actions were downright reckless. You could have easily taken your own life, or that of someone else," he remarks harshly.

"Yes, sir," I offer a simple and obedient response.

"Your license is gone. I'm suspending it for five months," he starts and I wince. This time the reaction isn't from the physical pain, but because the very thought of losing my freedom to ride is crushing.

"And finally, I'm remanding you to thirty days in Rock Hill jail. It's my sincere hope that this will give you some time to clear your head and consider where you really want your life to go. You're still a young man and this accident could have easily resulted in very tragic outcomes. It was senseless and completely irresponsible, but that being said, I think it can also be used as a learning opportunity," he finishes his lecture as I continue to nod along, the numbness taking over.

"Do you understand your sentencing as I've just explained it to you?" he asks.

"Yes, sir," I echo my previous statement.

"Okay then," he nods to the guard who approaches without hesitation. The cold metal cuffs close around my wrists and I glance back over my shoulder.

I lock on Cora's shocked, wide eyes as her hands lift to cover her open mouth. I'm not sure why Ryder brought her here for this, but knowing the little spitfire that she is, she probably wouldn't take no for an answer. I turn my attention to my Pres., tipping my head in his direction to let him know that I'm good and I can handle this. His face is stone, but he nods back in unspoken understanding.

I fucking understand. I know I got damn lucky making it through that accident without hurting anyone else. If that had been the case, I'd be facing years of my life gone, along with an endless supply of guilt to match.

But thirty fucking days…

Chapter Fifteen

Ayla

I'm not exactly sure where the past month went, but my summer turned into a complete blur. I stayed for a couple weeks with Dad after the trip to South Carolina, but eventually I knew I needed to go back to the apartment.

The first few nights alone were rough. There were still too many memories of Kane. I even spent one of my many sleepless nights rearranging the furniture in hopes that it would help. It didn't. And time has only helped a little. Most nights he still finds me in my dreams.

But today I'm wide awake and refreshed as I head towards campus. It's my first day back for my last semester. I can't believe I'll actually be done in December. I guess taking a few college level courses while I was still in high school, and a few extra classes my freshman year really made a difference. I'm more than ready to be done.

My phone beeps in the center console and I tap the button on the dash to listen to the message through the speakers. **Have a great first day back at school!*

It's Cora having a little fun with me. Normally we'd be making this drive together. She decided to hold off on starting back at school, she hasn't had enough time to check out her options in South Carolina.

When I talked to her a few days ago, she told me that Kane is getting out this week. He had never had a DUI before, but because of his previous record and the fact that he was double the legal limit, they gave him the maximum sentence for a first-time offense. He's spent the past thirty days behind bars.

He actually tried to call me once, but I didn't recognize the number so I didn't answer. He left a quick message telling me he was sorry and that he hoped I would talk to him when he got out. At first, I thought thirty days might give me enough time, but now that it's here I'm not sure I'll be able to handle it.

I fell for him, so hard and so fast and it's still there, lingering deep in my heart. And I want to see him, to hear his voice and let him hold me in his arms again. Then I remember how he hurt me and the anger comes back. Sometimes you have to walk away and keep that distance to protect yourself, and that's just what I'm trying to do.

I reach the exit for Plymouth State and pull off the highway, quickly finding a parking spot at the field house. It's a long walk to my classes, but it's not too bad on these warm sunny days. I grab my phone from the cup holder and type a quick response to Cora before climbing out of the car.

**Thanks! I miss having my driving partner. I had to sing all the songs myself.*

It vibrates in my back pocket as I start my walk. I slip it back out and hold my hand up to shade the screen as I read her response. **Miss you too. Have you thought about Thanksgiving?*

She had asked me to think about coming to South Carolina for Thanksgiving, and I've been stalling. I'm not ready to go there yet. As I walk, I type, **I think I'm going to stay home with Dad. He's got a new GF. I'll give you details later.*

Her reply comes through instantly, **Fine. But you have to promise to come for New Year's.*

Of course, she had to come back with some type of bargain. I need this to end so I can get to class, so I type back, **Deal. Xo*

Chapter Sixteen

Kane

God damn, it feels really good to be home. I stop and stand in my bedroom door. It's been a month but the memories are still fresh in my fucking mind. I look at the bed and the vivid images replay like it was yesterday.

The past thirty days away has given me nothing but time to think about her and what I should have done differently. But I can't go back, I don't get a do over. The best I can do is try to prove to her that she's all I want, that she's all I'll ever want, and hope that she'll listen.

I know I won't find shit, but I turn and head for the kitchen anyway. As I reach for the handle on the fridge, I notice a small piece of paper stuck to the surface, held up with a flat round magnet. I read the small handwritten note:

I thought you might need food.

Filled your fridge and cabinets.

Welcome home!

- Cora

I pull the fridge open, finding it stocked, complete with a case of Budweiser. I have the best fucking family. I reach in and pull out a bottle, quickly popping the top and tipping it back. Damn, that tastes like heaven. Half the bottle is gone in one swallow, and I reach in to grab another. Closing the fridge, I take both bottles and plant my ass on the worn leather couch. My phone lights up with an incoming text from Ryder.

**Welcome home! Club meeting in an hour and party after. Billy will be back to pick you up.*

Shit. Not sure I'm up for a welcome home party, but I type back a quick **sounds good.* I may not want to party, but I do want to see all my boys. As I stare at the screen, my eyes move over my messages with Ayla. The last messages between us were just over a month ago…

**I just heard about the accident. I'm glad you're okay.*

And my single word response, **Thanks.*

She was making a point to tell me she still cared, and despite all the things I wanted to say to her, I just couldn't do it in that moment and I definitely couldn't do it in a text. And that was the last word. I went away after that and while I disappeared the rest of the world kept moving for thirty days. I did try to call her once from inside, but I knew she wouldn't answer. I ended up leaving her some stumbling voicemail, probably sounding like a complete fucking fool.

I tap my thumb against the screen to start a new message, but I can't seem to find the right words. I drop the phone, letting it hit the couch cushions as I tip back the rest of my first bottle. Before I know it, the second one is empty too. I set it beside the first one, on the table in front of me, and I pick my phone back up. I push out a deep breath and let my fingers move.

**I got out today. I'm home. I know I have a lot to make up for, but you should know that I'm not giving up. I will have what's mine.*

I drop the phone again and lift my heavy body. I'm not going to wait around for a response I probably won't get, but at least I said what I needed to say. I move towards the bathroom, deciding I could use a nice hot shower before heading to the clubhouse.

I still can't believe I have to deal with Billy picking me up and driving me around. This shit is going to get really old, real fucking fast. Luckily, it's only a few months. Getting shit faced and trying to drive home definitely wasn't my finest hour of record.

As I walk through the bathroom door, I hear the faint beeping sound of an incoming text. I keep moving forward, knowing that it's probably just Fifty or one of the other boys welcoming me home. As much as I want it to be Ayla, I'm almost positive it's not her.

Just as I'm slipping into the familiar comfort of my leather cut, I hear a knock on the door. "Be right there," I holler from my room as I slip my ballcap down over my still damp hair. My boots stomp a path towards the door and I pull it open to find Billy's grinning face waiting for me. This kid is enjoying his new assignment as my driver way too much.

"Hey V.P., you ready to fuckin' party or what?" he chuckles quickly revealing the real reason behind the beaming smile.

"Yeah, kid," I answer as I turn back and quickly grab my phone and sunglasses. I slide my shades down to cover my eyes as I step outside and into the still blinding sunlight. I climb uncomfortably into the passenger side of Billy's rig, getting driven around is definitely going to take some getting used to.

"So, how do you feel about carting my sorry ass around?" I question as he backs into the road and starts to drive.

"It could be a lot fuckin' worse. It could be Shark," he shrugs and I can't help but chuckle.

"True," I laugh out the word as I let my eyes move to my phone, checking my missed texts. As expected, I find multiple messages from the boys, all welcoming me home. But then my eyes lock on one I wasn't expecting. Ayla responded.

My lungs burn in my chest suddenly feeling like I can't fucking breathe. I tap the screen and open her message.

**Good luck with that…* 😉

Holy shit.

Chapter Seventeen

Ayla

I read Kane's text about twenty times before I finally typed my response. Even with a text, he somehow has the ability to make me completely weak with just a few simple words. And I know…I am still his and I can already feel that familiar sensation deep in the pit of my stomach. I can't deny that I still want him.

I won't forget how he hurt me, but in all honesty, it wasn't just him. It was the whole situation. Everything between us happened so fast, and it wasn't really the typical start to a relationship. We dealt with big, life changing stuff. I ended my engagement with Ethan, and fell hard for Kane. Add in the pregnancy and it was bound to explode. It was just too much.

I mean, I don't want to make excuses for him because I still think how he reacted was wrong, but Kane lives in a different world. His life with the club is not the same as the quiet life I live in New Hampshire. Sure, working bike week every June is fun and I get a small taste of it, but that's all it is, a very small taste. He lives that every single day. The partying and the girls, I feel sick just thinking about it, but that's what he knows.

Our relationship was still so new, and me dropping the news about the baby was just enough to push him past the breaking point. When I think about his reaction and what he did, it definitely still stings, but I've had some time to clear my head and think about everything that happened between us. It's hard to admit, but I understand why he reacted the way he did. But just because I can see his side of it, it doesn't mean I'm going to cave and let him right back in.

I do, however, realize that he now has an inside advantage. He has my best friend in his ear. And even though she is completely loyal to me, I know that Cora wants to see us back together. She has dreams of me moving to South Carolina too, and I can guarantee that she'll be giving him anything he needs to try to win me back. I'm also fully aware that I have a weakness when it comes to Kane. Something about him just makes my insides melt, and with Cora spoon feeding him, I'll have to be extra cautious.

I try to focus back on my Chromebook but I just can't get back into my assignment. My mind is completely spinning after that text and it's impossible to concentrate. I save my file and shut it down, then push it off to the side. I lift my knees, curling them up on the seat cushions as I lean back into the couch. I lift my phone and once again let my eyes move over the screen to read his message, **I got out today. I'm home. I know I have a lot to make up for, but you should know that I'm not giving up. I will have what's mine.*

I will have what's mine.

My body heats as my imagination gets the best of me and those last five words echo in my mind. I hear his deep and cocky voice, perfectly clear, as if he was right next to me and whispering it against my ear. If he was here, I would cave.

The phone buzzes against my palm, startling me from my daze, and I see an incoming call from Cora.

"Hey. This is a surprise," I answer lightly.

"I know…I know, but I miss my bestie. I mean, everyone down here is super nice but it's just not the same," she whines against my ear.

"You're the one who moved," I remind her with a soft laugh.

"Ugh. Be nice. You sound like my mom," she groans. "Speaking of my mom, my parents decided to make the trip down here for Thanksgiving. Are you sure I can't convince you to come with them?" she pushes.

"I already told you that I can't," I shake my head even though I know she can't see me. "I think Dad and I are going to spend Thanksgiving with his new lady friend," I share. I still can't believe that my dad actually started dating someone. Her name is Wendy, and she seems to be over at the house every time I stop by lately. It's actually super cute and I'm happy that he's found someone to spend his free time with.

"I honestly can't believe that your dad never dated before," Cora replies. "I mean, I know he's like older, but he's pretty good looking and he's a cop. Isn't that like a turn on for some women?" she giggles.

"Gross. Can we please not talk about that aspect of my dad's relationship with his new girlfriend," I cringe and her laughter fills my ear. I can't help the smile that pulls at my lips hearing the happy sound.

I love that even with the distance between us we can still be like this when we're on the phone together. It's like she's still here with me. God, I miss her.

"Baby, are you almost ready?" I hear Ryder's voice through the phone.

"I'm on the phone with Ayla. Give me two more minutes," I hear her muffled reply. "I'm sorry about that. He's been in a mood today," she comes back to me.

"Do you want me to set him straight?" I joke.

"No. He really hasn't been that bad. Most of it's me and my fucking hormones. I started my period this morning and I've been missing home a little, which I think has him on edge. He's already been stressed, trying to handle all the club business himself while Kane was away. I'm hoping now that Kane's out that Ryder will relax a little and realize that I'm not going to go running home just because I miss my mom and dad, and you," she tells me.

"You know I miss you too, and I will come visit, just not for Thanksgiving," I promise her, suddenly realizing just how alone she is in her new home. She's in a new place, surrounded by a whole new family and I'm sure the adjustment hasn't been easy, no matter how much she loves Ryder. "So, what are you getting ready for?" I ask trying to move past the lingering emotion I know we're both trying to contain.

"The guys are having a welcome home party for Kane tonight," she shares.

I swallow hard, thinking of the remnants I found after the party they had while I was there. I can't help but wonder if he'll just fall right back into the routine. It's easy to send a text from a thousand miles away.

Just because he typed the words it doesn't mean he actually means them or plans to follow through. By the end of the night, he could be back in that room with that same girl…

"I guess maybe I should let you go finish getting ready," I force myself to say the words.

"Are you okay?" she asks quickly sensing my change in tone.

"I'm fine. Don't worry about me, you have enough going on," I tell her.

"It's Kane…and the party. Shit. I'm sorry. I shouldn't have said anything," she says.

"No, it's okay. I really am fine. It's not even an issue. I want you to go out and have fun tonight with Ryder and the boys. I'm happy that Kane is home and back with his family, his brothers," I feel my bottom lip tremble slightly as my words touch the air. She takes a deep breath and I bite down on my lip, trying to make it stop, already knowing what she's going to say next.

"You should be here. He still loves you," her words sink deep into my chest.

"He says he does, but it's not that simple or that easy," I breathe out. "I really wish it was," I admit.

Chapter Eighteen

Kane

"Best day of the fuckin' year boys," I grin, unable to keep the smile off my face. I fucking love Thanksgiving. Every year we have a huge spread at the club house and I eat more than anyone should ever consume. All the ladies get together and cook up the side dishes and desserts while the boys and I fry up turkeys out in the lot. I've been looking forward to this for months. There's only one thing I'm missing. I wish Ayla was here.

I thought after my thirty days away she'd be more open to talking to me, and I've tried. I've texted and I've called, but she's only texted back twice. She was the only thing I thought about while I was inside and she's all I want now, but she's still keeping me at a distance and despite the front I put on for the boys, I feel fucking broken without her.

Since I got out, I haven't been partying as much. Thirty days without Jack Daniels in my system helped clear my head. And I actually started working out and lifting weights again, which has helped burn off some of my pent-up sexual frustration. But today, I'm letting loose. Not with girls, but with my boys. I plan to thoroughly enjoy the holiday, and all the food and drink that go along with it.

"Fucking A. I love Thanksgiving," Fifty grins beside me, a cloud of smoke billowing from his mouth. He lifts his arm in my direction, offering me a hit. I take it. Why the fuck not. Like I said, I'm going to celebrate today.

I inhale deeply, letting the smooth smoke fill my lungs. I hold it for a second before finally letting it seep back out, then I do it again before holding it back out for Fifty to take.

"Fuck. That is good shit," I breathe out with the smoke.

"Yeah, it is. It's some of the stuff the boys brought back from Arizona. Ryder wanted us to make sure it was as good as the last batch. I think this might be even better," he grins bringing it back to his lips to take another drag.

"Let me get some of that," Mickey steps up beside me, followed closely by Army, Shark and Billy. I watch as they each take a hit before I get it back between my fingers.

"Food's almost ready boys," Carrie, Big E.'s ol' lady calls out across the lot. "Are you fucking kidding me right now? I can smell that shit all the way over here," she scolds and we all bust out laughing. "Assholes," she mutters before heading back inside letting the clubhouse door close behind her.

Two full plates of food down and I'm debating on whether or not to get more mashed potatoes, when a small plate with a slice of pie slides slowly in front of me. Cora sits down beside me with a big grin.

"I made it. It's my first time actually baking something, so I need a taste tester," she says.

"It's not fucking poisoned, is it?" I question with a deep chuckle.

"Don't be an asshole. I came over here to be nice to you," she throws back. I lift my fork and stab into the pie, lifting it to my mouth.

"God damn. That is fucking delicious," I announce as I chew, digging in for another forkful and she smiles brightly.

"Really? Or are you just saying that because of all the weed?" she laughs softly beside me.

"No. It's really fucking good. I could probably eat the whole pie," I tell her.

"I've never been much of a baker, but my mom gave me the recipe so I gave it a shot," she shares.

"Were your parents disappointed that you weren't coming home for Thanksgiving?" I ask.

"Actually, they were supposed to make the trip down here, but they got hit with an early snowstorm and they're flight got cancelled. They're still coming, but they won't be here until Saturday," she offers before turning to look at me. "But is that who you really want to hear about? My parents?" she questions knowing that when I ask her about going home, what I'm really thinking about is Ayla.

"How is she?" the question is a whisper across my lips.

"Actually…" she hesitates and I feel my body tense. "She's doing okay," she finishes her thought without really giving me anything at all.

"I tried texting her earlier," I admit.

"She'll come around. She just needs some time," she offers as her hand gently pats my arm.

"Hey! Stop trying to steal my girl," Ryder's deep laugh hits me from behind. He steps up, lowering his large body to wrap his arms around Cora's shoulders. "How're you doing, sweetheart," he drawls out in a soft voice close to her ear.

"I'm good. I made Kane act as my taste tester, and he's still alive and not puking, so I guess that's a good sign," she giggles.

"Well, I brought you a little treat," he tells her.

"A treat? What is it?" her face lights up.

His hand dives deep into his pocket, and in split second he's on the floor holding a small red box. Her eyes go wide and her hand lifts to cover her mouth. Is he really doing this?

"Cora, my life changed the day I met you. And I can't imagine spending a single day without you. I need you by my side, every day, every minute… Will you marry me?" he asks as the whole room goes silent around us. Her hands wave frantically in front of her face as she stares back at him in surprise.

"Yes…yes!!! Of course, a million times, yes!!" she leaps from her seat, crashing into him and almost knocking him completely to the floor. The room erupts with excitement.

"Woohoo! Fuck yeah! Congratulations!" the voices echo from

around the room. I stand, gripping Ryder's hand once Cora finally releases him.

"Congrats, brother," I pull him in and slap his back hard.

"You know you're next," he grins with a laugh.

"Oh, fuck no," I laugh back.

"Oh my God…I have to go call my mom, and Ayla. I can't even believe this!" Cora squeals bouncing around the room like she's on springs.

"Why don't you go on back to the bedroom and make all the calls you need to make," Ryder suggests the broad smile still filling his face. She lifts to her toes and kisses his cheek before disappearing down the hallway.

"I wasn't kidding when I said that you're next," Ryder says, turning in my direction. I shake him off, there are no wedding bells in my future without Ayla. "She'll be back. Cora will want her help with wedding plans," he offers as if reading my mind.

Chapter Nineteen

Ayla

"Wow, twice in one day. You're making me feel special," I answer when I see Cora calling again. I already talked to her this morning. She must be missing home with it being her first big family holiday away from home.

"I'm engaged!" her high-pitched excitement filled voice pierces my ear.

"Wait, what?" I question slowly before it finally hits me. "Oh my God! Congratulations! Tell me everything," I beg.

"Oh, Ay, it was completely perfect. I was sitting with Kane after dinner, forcing him to try the pie I baked, and Ryder snuck up behind me…and before I knew it, he was down on his knees and holding a ring," she gushes.

"I can't even believe it. Ryder actually got down on one knee?" my lips curl into a smile as the question comes out.

"He did, and it was amazing. You should have seen it," she says and I can hear the smile in her voice clinging to every word.

"I wish I had," I tell her. And I do wish I had been there to see it. I should have been there.

"As soon as we get through Christmas, I'm going to need you. Weddings take time to plan, and you have to help," she stresses.

"Holy shit. Is Cora engaged?" a surprised voice questions in my open ear, and I offer a small nod.

"Who is that?" Cora's voice comes through the phone. Shit.

"Hey, I'm going to leave. I just wanted to drop off the pie and say Happy Thanksgiving," Ethan whispers and I nod again as I mouth *thank you* and offer a small wave. I watch as Dad walks him over to the door.

"Thank your mom for me," Dad offers closing the door quickly behind him. I was not expecting a visit from Ethan, and now I have to try to explain this to Cora.

"Please don't tell me that is Ethan?" Cora's annoyance comes through as she waits for my answer.

"It was, but he's leaving," I start. "He was only here for about five minutes. His mom remembered how much my dad loves pecan pie. She made an extra one and sent him over to deliver it. I think she thought we'd be alone for Thanksgiving, not realizing that Dad's in a relationship now," I start to pour out, feeling the need to explain every tiny detail.

"Do not even think about going back to him. I swear, I will get on the next plane back to New Hampshire," she threatens and I know it's not to be taken lightly. She wouldn't hesitate to hop on a plane if she thought it was a real possibility. I stand from my seat on the couch and start to move towards my old bedroom for a little more privacy.

"Twenty minutes, then we're leaving for Wendy's," Dad's voice calls after me down the hallway. He's known Cora for long enough to know just how much she can talk. I close the bedroom door and sit lightly on the edge of my old bed.

"You know I could never go back to Ethan. I still…" my voice cracks and I stop. I can't bring myself to say the words out loud even though they're right on the tip of my tongue. Even after the way he hurt me, I just can't let go. I'm still in love with Kane. I feel my lip start to tremble, as it usually does when I start to think about him too much.

"Hey, this is supposed to be a happy call. Don't start crying on me. Maybe you should just talk to him and stop avoiding his calls," she pushes again, as she does almost every time I talk to her lately. Unfortunately, it's easier said than done. So many times, I've seen his name on the screen and wanted to pick up and answer, but the fear and anxiety consume me in the moment.

"Is that Ayla?" I hear Ryder's muffled voice in the distance.

"I'm putting you on speaker," Cora announces.

"Happy Thanksgiving, baby girl. Did Cora tell you the good news?" he asks excitedly.

"She did. Congratulations!" I offer feeling the smile spread on my face.

"So, you're coming back down here, right? We'll pay your way and you can stay in the guest room. Cora's gonna need your help with all the planning. You know I can't be held responsible for all that girly shit," he laughs deeply.

"I'll definitely help if I can," I offer without really committing myself to anything specific.

"We can work all that out later," Cora adds and I know she's letting me off easy because she's in a really good mood and it's a holiday.

"Hey, Ryder. The prospect found that champagne in the cooler. He's ready to pop it open whenever you are," I hear Kane's deep voice and my whole body reacts. My heart jumps to my throat and my stomach twists, while my deep muscles clench and I feel the heat pulse between my thighs, all at the sound of his voice.

"Just give us another minute to finish up this call," Ryder responds roughly.

"Oh, shit. Sorry. I didn't realize you were still on the phone," Kane's voice touches me again and a small shiver moves through my body.

My hand lifts to cover my mouth as my eyes move to the ceiling. I feel the glaze coating my eyes as I try to keep the tears at bay. I pull a deep breath in through my nose and let my hand fall away from my face.

"Cora, it's okay. You should go and celebrate. Go toast your champagne, and drink an extra glass for me. My dad and I have to get going anyway," the words rush out with my breath. "Happy Thanksgiving, Kane," I push out the last few words knowing that he can hear me through the speaker phone.

"Ayla, wait…" I hear Cora and Kane say in unison, but I can't. Having a conversation with him right now would be impossible. Hearing his voice was enough to turn me into a puddle. I tap the screen and end the call, letting the warm tears run over my cheeks.

Chapter Twenty

Kane

Why did I wait so long? I should have done this months ago. Oh yeah, that's right…I fucked up and lost my license so I didn't have much of a fuckin' choice other than to wait.

My knuckles turn white as I grip the steering wheel, knowing I'm getting close. My stomach has been twisted in a knot the whole ride, unsure how this is going to go. But I knew, the second I overheard Cora and Ryder talking, that this was my shot. It took some convincing, but Cora finally agreed. And now it's time to take my chance. No more waiting.

It's already dark, but I can see her car sitting in the driveway as I turn the corner. This was the only other place I knew to look when I didn't find her at the apartment. I pull in behind her car and shift the truck into park, cutting the engine.

I pull in a deep breath, giving myself an extra minute. I told her I wasn't giving up, but I don't think she's expecting me to show up at her door. I grip the handle and pop the door open, letting my boots hit the icy pavement. My breath instantly fogs into a faint white vapor, rising like smoke in the air.

God damn. It's fucking cold.

The truck door closes with a loud bang behind me. I start to walk, rubbing my hands together as I move quickly towards the house. I'm five feet from the steps when the front door flies open and Mr. Winters steps out in full fucking uni. Jesus Christ, *really?*

"What are you doing here?" he roars. "Don't take another step unless you want me to call some of my friends," his eyes darken on me. I raise my hands in defense.

"I know, I know. But I need to see her," I say truthfully.

"The fuck you do. I think you did enough damage the last time, don't you?" he rips right into me.

"I'm here to try to make up for that. I know I screwed up, but I need a chance to prove to her that I've changed. I love her and I…I need her," I admit, pushing out a heated breath and watching it swirl in the cold air between us.

"Well, I heard you had some time to think about what you did. Thirty days, does that sound about right?" he asks with a smirk only a cop could pull off.

"Yes sir, I did. That was another mistake. But you're right, it gave me plenty of time to think about Ayla and what I did to her. And I know I haven't known your daughter for long, but I also know that I want her in my life, and I was hoping by coming here that she'd at least talk to me," I answer.

I watch as he lifts his hand, rubbing it back and forth over his head as he works to make his decision. He clears his throat and finally lifts his eyes to look at me again.

"Here's the deal. I'll let you in because you seem to have good intentions and I'm sure you're freezing your ass off out here," he chuckles softly. "But if I see anything, and I mean anything, that I don't like I'll put you back out so fast your head will be spinning. And if my daughter asks you to leave, then you walk the fuck out. I don't want to hear any bullshit arguments or excuses, got it?"

"Yes, sir. I got it. Thank you," I reply. Right now, I'll take any chance I can get.

"Well, come on in then," he turns to move back towards the door.

The warm air tingles against my chilled skin as I step into the house. The scene inside is familiar, with the exception of a small glowing Christmas tree and a few scattered holiday decorations. My eyes are drawn to a puffy snowman pillow propped up on the couch.

"She's in the shower. Do you want a beer while you wait?" he questions, already reaching into the fridge and pulling out two cans.

I take one from his outstretched hand and crack it open, slowly pouring it back. I drove all the way here and now the nerves are kicking in something serious. A little liquid courage can't hurt.

"So, did you spend all Christmas day driving?" he asks.

"Yup. I drove almost straight through," I tell him. I did stop a couple times just to rest my eyes in the truck and use the bathroom along the way, but I couldn't stop for long. Once I was on the road, my intense need to see her took over completely. Food and sleep took a backseat. Nothing else mattered; I just needed to get here. The water stops running, easily getting my attention, and I tip my beer back feeling my chest tighten.

"So, Ayla told you what happened in South Carolina?" I ask, wondering how much he actually knows.

He brings his beer to his lips, taking a long drink before setting the can down on the counter. He pulls in a deep breath as his eyes lift to the ceiling before finally settling in on me.

Shit.

"She did. But I know my daughter, and I'm sure what she told me was a watered-down version of the truth," he starts before picking the can back up and taking another large swallow. He moves from the kitchen into the living room and plants himself in his recliner, reaching for the remote. He flips the TV on and the local news blares between us as he quickly lowers the volume.

"My daughter came back from that trip a different person. She's been quiet and has spent way too much time inside her own head. It's been hard to watch, but she's a grown woman and I had to step back and let her work through it in her own way," his words are crushing. My stomach curls and I feel sick just thinking of the pain I caused her. I don't know if she'll ever forgive me.

"It sounds like she's out of the shower," he says, standing from his chair when the sound of doors opening and closing echoes down the hallway. "I'll go let her know she has a visitor, that way she isn't too surprised," he starts to move and I feel the tightness spreading. I can't fucking breathe.

"She needs a little time, so just give her another minute," he offers, returning only minutes later. "I think she might be in shock, but she said she'll come out and talk to you. I'm going to go in my room and give the two of you a little privacy, but I won't be too far. Remember what I said. If she asks you to leave, then you leave," he reminds me.

"Yes, sir," I nod.

"Good luck, son," a slight grin pulls at his lips before he turns away and walks back down the darkened hallway.

Did he really just wish me luck? And did he call me son? Shit, he might actually be rooting for me. A fresh heat floods my skin as I realize maybe this means this trip wasn't all for nothing. Maybe I actually still have a shot with her.

I start to pace back and forth in the small living room, finally stopping beside the soft glowing lights on the Christmas tree. I watch as they blink on and off in a timed cycle, reflecting off all the glass ornaments hanging on the tree. Normally I'd be with my parents and sister, but this year the only person I wanted to be with was Ayla. I hear a hushed breath behind me, and I feel my body stiffen knowing she's emerged.

I turn to face her and her beauty is unmatched. All my memories, and even the photos on my phone didn't do her justice. Her long chocolate hair falls damp against her shoulders, and she looks unbelievably sexy in a pair of leggings and a flannel shirt. Her wide eyes move over me as if she can't believe I'm here, even though her dad went in and gave her fair warning.

"Kane," my name passes her lips in a soft whisper and my knees just about buckle at the sound. But I pull in a deep breath and somehow manage to lift up taller.

"Merry Christmas, sweetheart," I answer with a smile.

Chapter Twenty-One

Ayla

I can't believe it. Kane is actually here and standing in my dad's living room.

"What…what are you doing here?" I manage to ask.

"I needed to talk to you, and I wanted to see you. I thought maybe I could give you a ride," he smirks and my belly drops at the double meaning.

"A ride?" I stutter.

"Yeah. A ride to South Carolina for New Year's," he clarifies with a cock of his eyebrow.

"But Cora and Ryder… Oh—" I put it together as the words start to leave my lips. They set this all up. "Did they ever actually think about getting me a plane ticket, or was this the plan all along?" I ask.

"They did. You really shouldn't blame them. I talked them into letting me do this. I thought if we had a couple days in the truck together, that it would give us a chance to talk," his honesty seeps out.

"And if I say no?" I question softly.

"Then I'll pay for your plane ticket and your gas to drive to the airport," his lips curl into a smile that I can't ignore and I feel my cheeks flush. He is definitely charming when he wants to be.

I manage to make my legs move, walking towards the couch and taking a seat. It takes all my energy to appear relaxed and normal, even though my heart is beating so fast it feels like it might burst straight through my chest at any second.

"Okay," I breathe out the single word.

"Okay? Okay, what? Okay, you'll ride to South Carolina with me or okay, go ahead and call the airline?" his questions pour out. I can't help the giggle that escapes as I take in the look of absolute confusion on his face. He's supposed to be this tough, larger than life, V.P. to his motorcycle club, but the look on his face is like a little boy who can't find his favorite toy.

"Just come sit for a minute," I offer, patting the seat cushions beside me.

"Your tree is real," he says as he lowers his large body down on the opposite end of the couch. My body is buzzing with excitement having him so close after so much time spent apart. I can't deny that he awakens something deep within me, but I have to be cautious. My mind struggles, feeling like I should still be upset and angry after the way he hurt me, but at the same time feeling this overwhelming need to crawl into his lap.

"It is," I answer. "Dad gets a real one every year," I tell him.

"Shit. We only had a real one a few times. My parents bought a fake one years ago," he shares. "Do you come home every Christmas to stay with your dad?" he asks.

"I do," and as the words leave my mouth, it dawns on me. Instead of spending Christmas with his family and friends, he spent the entire holiday driving alone to New Hampshire, *for me…*

"Are you thirsty or hungry? Do you want a drink or something to eat?" I shift on the couch feeling myself start to crack now that I realize the weight of what he's done.

"No, thanks. I'm good. Your dad actually gave me a beer," he grins and my heart melts.

As a cop, my dad has always been on the more protective side, especially when it came to boys and dating. But even after I came home from South Carolina, I knew he had a soft spot for Kane. Those first few weeks, months even, I felt so lost. My heart was broken and Dad had to watch me fall apart. Of course, he would curse Kane's name and threaten bodily injury, but he knew, just as well as I did, that despite all the hurt, I still love this man sitting in front of me.

"I can't believe you spent Christmas in your truck driving here," I finally breathe out recognizing his gesture.

"It was worth it," he smiles and I feel the glassiness spreading over the surface of my eyes. "Sweetheart, please don't cry," his voice softens and my eyes drop to my lap. His large hand reaches to touch my chin.

"Please look at me. It's hard enough being this close to you and not being able to touch you, but when you look at me like that it's pure fucking torture," he says. And with that, I'm completely done for. My body trembles and I clamp down on my bottom lip to stop the sob that's fighting to break free.

Kane inches closer, until I can feel his warmth drawing me in. His thick biceps move around me and I lean into him, breathing in his strong scent. He mirrors me, and inhales deeply before pushing out a ragged breath.

"Ayla, I love you. Please…please give me this chance to prove to you that this is all I want, all I need. One chance, that's all I'm asking for, just one. And then, if you still hate me, I'll leave you alone," he begs.

"I don't hate you. I could never…" my voice shakes but he stops me before I can finish.

"Shhh. You don't need to explain. I'm the one who fucked everything up and I'm sorry," his voice is raw with honesty and another small sob pulls at my chest.

"Okay, I'll let you drive me to South Carolina," I pull back, wiping the warm tears away with the back of my hand.

"Really?" he questions, the surprise clear on his face.

"Yes, really," I confirm with a small nod. "Where were you planning to stay tonight?" the question slips from my lips.

"I figured I'd just get a room at the Naswa," he shares and my mind flashes with memories from bike week.

"You're welcome to stay here for the night," I offer. "I mean, you can sleep on the couch, and then we can leave in the morning," I clarify.

"Yeah…yeah. As long as you're really okay with it?" he double checks and I know without a doubt that I am. I've avoided him for too long; definitely longer than I should have. But as much as I wanted to let him back in, I was so hurt and I guess I wanted him to hurt too. I know we both have things on our minds, things we want to say. I think riding with Kane to South Carolina will finally give us the chance we both need.

Chapter Twenty-Two

Kane

My fingers curl around the hard white edge of the counter as I stare at myself in the mirror above the bathroom sink. I inhale, taking a deep cleansing breath. Fuck. I had to use the excuse of needing to take a piss to get a minute alone and try to calm myself down. Being so close to her is seriously fucking with my mental state.

She let me hold her and she agreed to let me drive her to South Carolina. My body is shaking as the adrenaline pumps through my veins. I push out another breath, trying to contain my excitement. I need to get a fucking grip before I go back out there.

She offered to order a pizza, and told me I can crash on the couch. It's not the same as sharing a bed with her, but it's a step in the right direction. And she said she doesn't hate me. Shit, if I was in her place, I'd fucking hate me. She's giving me a chance. One that I probably don't really deserve. Now I'll have two days; two days alone with her to convince her that I'll never hurt her again.

I push up off the counter and lift up taller, trying to fuel my confidence. I finally turn the doorknob and force myself to step out of the bathroom. I find her sitting on the couch, her legs curled up underneath her body. She looks up at me and I pause, just to take in the sight of her. Feeling her in my arms again was fucking incredible and I can't give that up. She's mine and I want her back.

"I ordered a pizza. It should be here in about fifteen minutes," she flashes a soft smile.

"Thanks, I'm actually fucking starving," I admit now that some of my initial stress has started to pass.

"You can sit back down," she offers and I don't hesitate. If she's going to invite me to sit with her, I'm doing it without question. I sit, leaving about a foot of space between us. I want to give her space, but that's about my limit when she's this close. I watch as she starts pressing the buttons on the remote, flipping through the channels, but I don't even bother to see what she stops on. I can't take my eyes off her.

"So, does everyone know you're here?" her question is a whisper.

"Actually, no. Obviously, Ryder and Cora know, but no one else in the club knows. They all think I'm with my family for Christmas," I tell her. I couldn't tell the boys about this trip. Losing her, and the aftermath that followed was the biggest fuck up of my life, and they all bore witness. If they knew that I made the drive to New Hampshire just to have her reject me, it would fucking destroy me. My own feelings of failure would be bad enough. There's no way I'd survive the never ending looks of pity. They'd never truly respect me again. And I wouldn't have anyone to blame but myself. So, I kept it from the boys.

"What about your family? Aren't they upset that you weren't there for Christmas?" she asks.

"They forgave me pretty quick once I told them what I was doing," I share and her eyes go wide. I had to tell my mom and Leia. Missing Christmas wasn't something to be taken lightly, so they had to know the real reason.

"So, your family knows about me?" her voice is soft and I nod in confirmation. I have no doubt, my mom and sister will love her almost as much as I do.

"Maybe some time you'll want to meet them," I offer as casually as possible, but I hear her breath catch in response. Shit. I went too far. I tip my head slightly, trying to gauge her reaction from the corner of my eye.

"That would actually be nice...I mean, to see where all *this* came from," she grins, as her hand lifts in the air, moving in a small circle in front of me.

"Oh really?" I throw back, loving the fact that she's getting playful. The doorbell rings, interrupting our moment and she lifts easily from her seat.

"That must be our pizza," she moves towards the door.

My eyes are locked on the ceiling, staring up into the darkness. I've tried closing them, but it's no fucking use. There is no way I'll be sleeping tonight.

The past few hours with her, just sitting together on this couch, have been unbelievable. I know it's still early, but being near her and seeing her smile has given me a renewed sense of hope. God damn, even in my own head I sound like such a fucking pussy, but I will literally crawl at her feet if that's what it will take. I will do anything for her. This woman owns me.

The screen on my phone lights up, creating a soft glow throughout the room. I reach for it and see a new message from Cora.

**I know you have to be there by now. What's going on?? I haven't heard from her. Is she pissed at me for letting you do this?*

Sounds like she freaking the fuck out. I let my fingers move over the screen.

**I'm here. She's giving me a chance. We're leaving in the morning. Chill the fuck out because I'm trying to sleep.*

I set my phone back on the coffee table and roll to my side, facing the back of the couch. Knowing Cora, there will be a response or two…or three, and I don't feel like dealing with that shit right now. I let my eyes close but I don't expect to actually sleep. I just need to try to rest before the start of our drive tomorrow.

My eyes open and I lift to roll over, hearing movement. A faint light spills from the kitchen and I can hear the trickle of the coffee maker. Fuck. I must've actually fallen asleep. I reach my heavy arm out, tapping the screen on my phone where it still sits on the coffee table. The time shows on the screen as six thirty, and I'm shocked to see that Cora never responded. I leave it on the table, as I slip off the edge of the couch and out from under the throw blanket Ayla gave me to stay warm. My arms stretch up over my head, my hands grazing the rough popcorn ceiling with my fingertips as I feel the stretch down through my back.

"Shit, I didn't mean to wake you," Mr. Winters offers as I step into the light of the kitchen.

"No worries," I shrug. I never expected to sleep anyway, so the couple hours I got were enough.

"How was the couch?" he raises an eyebrow.

"Not bad," I grin back, knowing that he's tiptoeing around the fact that I didn't sleep with his daughter last night. If he only knew the things I've done to her body, but I'll let him enjoy this moment.

"You want a cup?" he asks, gesturing towards the coffee pot.

"Yeah, sounds good. Smells really good," I reply. "You heading to work?" I ask, noticing his uniform.

"Soon. I've got about a half hour or so before I need to leave. Ayla tells me that you'll be leaving later this morning," he says.

"Uh…yeah. Once she's up and ready to go. She mentioned stopping at her apartment to grab a few things, but then we'll be on our way," I explain.

"She'll be checking in with me regularly," he says, handing me a steaming mug. "My rules still apply for the road. If she asks to come home, you let her come home," his voice is steady and I know he means every word.

"Yes, sir," I nod.

"Is this your Sig?" he questions checking out my holster sitting on the kitchen table, my cut hanging close by on the back of one of the chairs.

"Yes, sir," I repeat.

"That's a nice piece," he steps back, taking a sip from his mug.

"What do you carry?" I question out of curiosity.

"Day to day, my service piece is a Glock twenty-two, but for personal protection I have a Sig myself. I've actually done a little training at the Sig Sauer facility," he shares.

"Really? That's fuckin' sweet," my excitement is genuine and he grins back.

"Yeah, they actually have a pretty nice set up here in New Hampshire. It's down in the southern part of the state, and they have a shitload of training options," he shares. "Shit. I guess I better get a move on," he says noticing the time. He sets his mug in the sink and disappears back down the hallway.

I take my mug and move back towards the couch, blowing across the top before taking a small sip. I take a seat and grab the remote off the coffee table. I hit the power button to turn it on and immediately hit the button to turn the volume down, as the soft light from the TV screen fills the room. The heavy footsteps coming down the hallway get my attention.

"I went in to say goodbye to her, but she's still half asleep. Make sure she either calls or texts me before you guys leave. And I'm sure I don't have to say this, but I'm going to say it anyway. Keep her safe. The second you leave in that truck she becomes your responsibility and I expect you to protect her," he says and I stand.

"I will, always," I promise as I reach out my hand for him to shake before watching him leave.

Stepping out of the bathroom, I pause catching sight of her standing in the living room. Her long brown hair melts softly down her back as she focuses her attention out the window, slowly sipping her coffee. She's been quiet since she came out of her room. I hope she's not second guessing her decision. I force out a breath before finally moving forward to join her.

"Are you almost ready?" I question and she turns, giving me a nod. Here we go. We're actually leaving here…*together.*

Present day

Chapter Twenty-Three

Ayla

I pick up my grilled cheese and take a big bite. I'm not sure why I'm so hungry, I've just been staring out the window of the truck for the most part. The first leg of our trip has been quiet. We've made some small talk, but I'm just too nervous to dive into the bigger stuff and Kane doesn't seem to want to bring it up either.

"That pie looks pretty damn good. Think you might want to split a piece with me?" he asks with a broad smile as he lifts his glass of coke and takes a long drink. I turn my head and let my eyes move over the glass case full of pies and cakes.

"Maybe. I guess it depends on the flavor," I give him a small smile and his eyes flash in a familiar fashion.

"Sweetheart, you keep smiling at me like that and I'll buy you a slice in every fuckin' flavor they've got," he cocks his eyebrow and a strong pulse pulls deep in my center. I turn my head again, trying to catch my breath, but my eyes stop on a booth across the diner.

It's a family sitting together and enjoying dinner. A man, woman and child sit together, talking and laughing like any other family. But there is something different about the woman and I can't seem to look away. It's weird, but she bears a resemblance to the old photos and faded memories of my mom. But it's been twelve years since she left us, there's no way it could be her. Still, I keep watching as she smiles at the little girl sitting next to her, and tucks her shoulder length hair back behind her ear.

I pull a breath through my teeth and clamp down on my bottom lip. It can't be…but it is. It's her. That small movement and her smile. Even after all these years, something in my brain knows. The woman in the corner booth is most definitely my mom.

"Ay…Ayla," Kane's deep voice breaks through. "Are you okay?" he asks and I'm barely able to acknowledge him. Her head snaps up at the sound of my name; it's not a common one and I know she heard him. My eyes drop not wanting her to see me. Kane's large hand reaches across the table and he lifts my chin to meet his worried gaze.

"What's wrong? Did I do something?" he questions and I melt at his sweetness, but I still don't want her to see me.

"It's not you. I…I think I need to leave," I barely get out a whisper, my voice failing me.

"What is it? Do you feel okay?" he asks and I shake my head, unable to find the words. It's too late. I can feel her eyes burning into me from across the room. I look up briefly and see them widen as she stares at me open mouthed, the shock clear on her face.

"That woman over there," I start. "I'm, uh…I'm pretty sure she's my mom," I finally breathe out the words lodged tightly in my throat. Kane turns, glancing over his shoulder before quickly turning back in my direction.

"I don't know, sweetheart. She could be anyone," he shrugs.

"No, Kane. I already thought she kind of looked like my mom, but then when you said my name. Her reaction gave it away. It's definitely her," I tell him.

"Okay, I need you to listen to me," his voice is steady. "Don't look at her. Just get up and go out to the truck and wait for me," he says handing me his keys.

I flatten my palms on the table and force myself to stand. I grab my coat and purse from the seat and as I turn, I make the mistake of taking one last look in her direction. She's still locked right on me, and now the man is looking too. Kane stands beside me, quickly blocking the path of vision.

"I'll take care of the check, then I'll be right behind you. Go ahead," his lips touch my ear and I nod, turning and moving hurriedly towards the door.

"Ayla!" I hear a woman's voice call my name as I push through the door, but I don't turn around. I walk straight across the parking lot and I don't stop until I climb into the safety of Kane's truck.

My eyes stare through the windshield and I can see her standing beside Kane in the diner window. I pull out my phone and find Dad under my contacts, hitting the call button. The phone rings loudly against my ear as my heart pounds against my chest. What am I going to tell him?

"Hey, Ayla," Wendy's cheerful voice answers. "How's the road trip going so far?"

"Hi, Wendy. Could I please talk to my dad?" I ask curtly. I don't want to be rude to her, but I can't pretend to do small talk right now.

"Sure, hun. Is everything okay?" she asks softly.

"No, not really. I just really need my dad," I manage feeling myself starting to crack.

"Okay, here he is," she says and I hear a few hushed whispers as the phone exchanges hands.

"Ay, what's wrong?" Dad's voice comes through and it gives me instant comfort. I know he's expecting the issue to be Kane, he'll never expect this.

"It's my mom…" I barely get the words out as hot tears begin to roll down my cheeks. I bite my lip to stop a sob from breaking through.

On a daily basis, I never give this woman much thought. She left. She made her choice. She chose drugs over her family. At different points in my life, it's made me sad or angry, but over the last few years I gradually just let her go. Cora's mom has been there for me, and Ethan's mom was there when we were together. But now, seeing her in person and appearing to be clean and sober with a whole new family, a new daughter, it's like a punch right to the stomach.

"What do you mean?" Dad's voice fills my ear and I pull a deep breath through my nose.

"We stopped to get food before finding a hotel for the night. We're just over the state line into Maryland, and she's here. I saw her, sitting in a booth across the diner," I try to explain, but I'm honestly not sure

I'm making any sense. I hear a heavy breath through the phone.

"No. After all these years, it can't be..." he mutters.

"I thought that at first too, but it is, Dad. She heard Kane say my name and she looked right at me. It's her," I try to convince him.

"I never...I never heard where she ended up. And she never made any attempt... I thought she was gone, lost to the drugs," he shares.

"I know," my voice is barely above a whisper.

"Wait. Where are you now?" his voice turns to worry.

"Kane's truck. He stayed inside the diner to pay the check, but I had to get out," I answer.

"I understand. You don't owe her anything," he says.

"I know, but... She was with a man, and a little girl. She has a new family," my lip trembles as the words pass through.

"Oh, Jesus. Ayla, I'm so sorry. Really, I don't even know what to say to that. I think you need to take a deep breath and try to calm down, and in all honesty, I'd feel much better if you stayed close to Kane tonight. I know that probably sounds strange, but honey, I don't think you should be alone tonight," he says clearly worried about me.

"Okay. Thanks, Dad. I love you," I offer.

"I love you too. And call me again if you need to, no matter the time," he tells me and I touch the end call button. Just as I disconnect, the driver's side door opens startling me slightly. Kane climbs in and hands me two small square boxes.

"I had a feeling you might need that pie after all," he offers lightly.

"That was her, wasn't it?" I question knowing that she said something to him after I ran out.

"Yeah, sweetheart. It was her," he confirms with a nod. "Let's get out of here. I think a hot shower and some sleep might help."

I turn and glance out the passenger side window, staring blankly into the darkness as we drive. Kane pulls the truck off the highway and into the parking lot of a Marriott. I'm sitting, still stunned in my seat when Kane opens my door and helps me from the truck. I watch as he pulls our bags from the back, and I start to follow him inside to the front desk.

"A single or double?" I hear the receptionist ask Kane as I stand quietly beside him, my brain in a complete fog.

"Double," he replies and I see him hold up two fingers.

"Okay. And how many nights will you be staying with us?" she asks.

"Just tonight," he answers.

"Great. I just need a major credit and you'll be all set," she requests as he's already handing her the small piece of plastic. It's obvious that he's been through this routine before. She smiles and types quickly on her computer before handing it back to him.

"You'll be in room three-oh-two," she says handing him a key card. She proceeds to explain how to get to the elevator and up to our room, but I've stopped listening. "Is there anything else I can help with?" she questions.

"No, ma'am. Thank you," his deep voice replies.

"Thank you. Have a nice night and enjoy your stay with us," I hear her voice but I've already turned away, staring at a small fountain trickling in the lobby.

"Come on, sweetheart," Kane's voice touches my ear and I turn to follow on his heels as he leads the way to our room.

Chapter Twenty-Four

Kane

Looking at Ayla, I want nothing more than to scoop her up and carry her, but I know I can't, not yet. She has to let me back in first. What a fucking disaster. This was the last thing I would have ever predicted.

And I can't believe her mother, if you can even call her that. The woman actually had the fucking nerve to give me her number to give to Ayla. What a fucking piece of work. Leave your husband and daughter so you can keep getting high, and then never call or attempt to make contact when you decide to get clean. I took the number, written on a napkin from the diner, and shoved it in my pocket. I'll give it to Ayla to do with it as she pleases, but definitely not tonight. My girl needs a minute to process this.

I unlock the door to our room and push it open, reaching inside to flip on the light before holding it open for Ayla to walk in. She moves slowly past me and sits on the edge of one of the large queen-sized beds filling the room.

"Maybe you should try a nice hot shower," I suggest and her eyes lift up, sweeping over me. She looks so broken and it's fucking killing me. She nods as I step closer, setting her bag down on the bed beside her. I watch as she unzips it and pulls out a smaller bag and some clothes.

I move across the room, stepping into the empty bathroom and flipping that light on too. I grab two large white towels off the shelf and set them on the countertop, ready for her to use. As I step back into the bedroom, she lifts from the bed with her things clutched in her hands.

"Take as long as you need," I offer as she moves past me and into the bathroom, closing the door behind her and leaving me alone in the room.

I grab my own bag from the floor and drop it on the empty bed. Pulling the zipper, I dig inside, searching for my bottle of Jack. I know it's hidden somewhere under all the clothes. I threw it in there before I left home. I knew I'd need it if Ayla refused to talk to me when I got to New Hampshire. I got lucky and haven't needed to crack it open yet, but I think we both might need a glass tonight.

My fingers finally grip the neck of the bottle, pulling it free from the bag. I hear the water turn on in the shower, and I decide to go in search for the ice machine, knowing that I've got at least a few minutes. I grab the small ice bucket from the table, and head back out into the hallway. It only takes a minute before I'm heading back to the room with a bucket full of ice.

As I push through the door, I hear Ayla's phone going off. It's sitting beside her bag on the bed. I move quickly to grab it, but it stops before I can get to it. Just as I turn back around, it starts ringing again. This time I see *'Dad'* flash on the screen, and I'm within reach. I pick it up and swipe the screen.

"Hello," I answer.

"Kane?" he questions.

"Yes, sir. We just got to the hotel and Ayla hopped in the shower, but I thought I should answer so you wouldn't worry," I explain.

"How's she doing? Is she okay?" his questions are heavy with concern. I push out a deep breath trying to figure out the best way to answer.

"Honestly, I don't know. She barely spoke when we left the diner. I'm hoping a hot shower and some sleep with help, but there's something else," I start. "Her mom, she came over and talked to me when Ayla walked out of the diner. She gave me her phone number to give to Ayla. She wants to talk to her," I tell him and he pulls in a sharp breath.

"Are you fucking kidding me? That woman left us, left us for her next fucking fix and never looked back. And now, through pure coincidence, her daughter gets dropped in front of her and she thinks that's an invitation to just walk right back in after twelve fucking years!" he fumes.

"I know," I offer a simple response, trying to give him a minute to cool off. "I haven't given it to her yet, but I will. She needs to be the one to make that decision."

"Shit, you're right. Sorry for going off on you like that. None of this is your fault, you're just caught in the crossfire," he apologizes. "Please, just keep an eye on her tonight," he requests.

"I will. I'll take care of her," I promise.

"I don't doubt that for a second," he replies and I feel my chest swell.

After ending the call, I set her phone back on the bed and return to my original mission of finding glasses. I separate the stacked glasses and drop a couple ice cubes in each. Twisting off the cap, I pour the amber liquid halfway up the side of the glass. I inhale the sweet scent as I bring it to my lips, intending to just take a small sip. Before I know it, the entire contents of the glass are gone in one swallow.

As I set the empty glass back down on the table, I hear the shower stop. I fill my glass again and grab the remote, taking a seat on the end of the bed and turning on the small TV. The bathroom door opens and the bright light floods into the bedroom as she steps back into the room. Her body is covered in a pair of black leggings and a cropped black tank, giving me the smallest peek at the smooth skin of her stomach. Her long brown hair falls damp on her shoulders as small droplets soak into her thin tank top. I can't help but stare. She is so fucking beautiful.

"Did the shower help at all?" I manage to ask.

"A little," her voice is soft. "Hey, did I hear you talking to someone?" she tips her head at me as she picks her bag up from the bed and drops it to the floor.

"Shit, yeah. I answered your phone, actually. Your dad called and I didn't want him to worry," I share.

"Should I call him back?" she asks.

"I think he's good, unless you really want to," I answer, standing from the bed and grabbing her glass off the table. "Here, this might help you get some sleep," I stretch my arm out, but her nose scrunches.

"You just happened to have this with you?" she questions taking the glass from my hand and immediately setting it down on the small night stand situated between the two large beds.

"Never leave home without it," I offer with a smile, and she finally cracks letting out a small giggle.

"What kind of pie did you get?" her lips curve into a smile and I have to stop myself from lunging at her. I clear my throat in search of my voice.

"Cherry, apple, and chocolate cream. I wasn't really sure what you'd be in the mood for, so I mixed it up," I tell her.

"Can I have the cherry?" she asks biting at her bottom lip.

"Sweetheart, you can have 'em all if you want," I grin in response before bringing my glass of Jack back to my lips to take a sip. I flip open the small containers, finding the cherry and apple wedged together. I grab one of the plastic forks, and hand it over to her.

"Do you mind if I eat the chocolate cream? It's my favorite, but I missed out on my mom's at Christmas," I share.

"Go ahead. I'm not going to eat three pieces of pie by myself," she smiles.

I grab my own fork and container of pie, and settle myself down on my bed. We both eat silently as we watch an old episode of *Friends*. I know the past couple hours have been rough, and I can't imagine what's going through her head, but it's nice to hear her laughing softly as she watches the TV.

I follow up my last bite of pie with a large swallow of Jack, emptying my glass for the second time. I stand from the bed and toss my empty container in the trash before heading towards the bathroom. I turn and look at her over my shoulder, and we make eye contact.

"Are you all set for a minute? I just want to hop in the shower to rinse off," I say.

"I'm good, go ahead," she says and I move into the bathroom, closing the door behind me. I'm quick, taking just enough time to wash my hair and do a quick scrub of my body. After drying, I slip into a pair of clean boxer briefs and move back into the bedroom.

The two small lights are now off, but the TV is still on and glowing in the dark room. The sound is turned down low, and Ayla is curled up in her bed. She's facing away from me, and her body looks tiny, only filling a portion of the large bed. As I step up to my bed and pull back the blanket, I notice that her glass is almost empty. I guess she decided she needed that drink after all.

I slip under the covers and lean back against the over fluffed pillows, trying to get comfortable, when I hear her take a deep breath. I thought she was asleep.

"Kane," her voice breaks and hearing my name on her lips excites me in a way I can't even begin to describe.

"Yeah?" I respond in question.

"Would you…would you sleep over here, with me?" her voice is soft and her words spiral around me, making me dizzy.

"Are you sure?" I can't help but ask, trying to keep my voice from giving me away.

"I'm sure. Please…" she whispers and this time I don't hesitate. I'm out of my bed and climbing into hers within seconds. Her warmth is inviting, and I pull a breath through my teeth, trying to keep myself calm as my heart pounds rapidly against my chest. I leave a small space between us, but she scoots back and my body vibrates at the contact. She doesn't turn to face me, but she reaches back and grabs my hand, lifting and pulling my arm up and over the side of her body. She keeps her hand clenched tightly with mine as my arm relaxes to hold her.

"Thank you," she breathes out. I lean in to her neck, feeling the warmth radiating from her skin. I can't help it; I crave her and being this close is almost more than I can handle.

"No need to thank me, sweetheart. I'm here any time you need me," I assure her with a whisper before placing one small kiss to her neck then relaxing back into my pillow. I will happily stay right here all night holding her, even if it means I don't get a single wink of sleep.

Chapter Twenty-Five

Ayla

His proximity has my senses on overload. The smell of the soap clinging to his skin and the sweet whiskey still lingering on his lips fill my nose with each breath. The heat from his body, now pressed firmly into my back, creates a smoldering fire over the surface of my skin. I want nothing more than to turn around and kiss him, hard and wild, letting the passion consume us both. But my brain won't let me. Somehow the rational thoughts have remained in charge, and I know if I let my body lead the way I'll just turn tonight into even more of a mess. Right now, I just need him to hold me.

My body sinks deeper in the softness of the mattress as I let my eyes close. The half a glass of whiskey that I drank has quickly made my head a little fuzzy. I let the warmth between us wash over me and I know it won't take long before I'm in a deep sleep.

The bed shifts, waking me. The room is dark and I'm not sure how long I've been asleep. My eyelids lift when I hear a small click, realizing that Kane got out of bed to go to the bathroom. I lift to my elbow and reach to tap my phone on the side table to check the time. It lights up, letting me know that it's just after one. I lie back and snuggle in, relaxing deeper under the blanket and letting my eyes close again.

I'm hovering at the edge of sleep but a dull repetitive noise fills my ears. Where is that noise coming from? What is that?

Wait.

Oh. My. God.

It's Kane, in the bathroom. Is he really doing what I think he's doing? I can't help but listen harder, and yes, there's no doubt. I can't believe he's taking care of himself in the bathroom right now. He has absolutely no idea that I'm awake in here, or how thin these hotel walls are.

A surprising, and familiar warmth rushes between my thighs as the realization hits me. He's in there because I asked him to share the bed with me tonight. A deep pulse vibrates through my core, and I squeeze my thighs trying to calm the ache. It's not like I can give myself the same level of gratification he's getting right now. I don't want to take the chance that Kane will walk back into the room and catch me mid-act. A dull groan echoes through the wall and my body shudders in response, remembering exactly how he felt every time he was inside me.

The water turns on briefly and then the door opens. I keep my eyes shut tight as he climbs back into the bed beside me. He shifts closer to me and I feel his soft lips touch my shoulder, creating a tingling sensation through my entire body.

"I love you," his voice is a soft whisper against my ear, and I bite my lip holding back my breath.

I listen as his breathing slows, quickly becoming deep and regular until I know he's asleep beside me. I roll gently to face him, letting my eyes adjust to the darkness as I watch him sleep. In the short time I've known him, Kane has managed to make me feel a full spectrum of emotions. And tonight, has been something different altogether. He's shown me how much he really does care, and I feel a tug deep in chest as a glassy coating covers my eyes. My feelings for him haven't changed. I love him and as I let my eyes close, I know it's time to let him back in.

The room is still dim when my eyes open again, and the first thing I see is Kane's bare chest. My eyes move over the intricate details of the black ink etched into his skin. I think about him sitting for hours at a time getting these tattoos and wonder what each one means to him, or if he'll get more. He clears his throat and I tip my head up towards his face, finding his eyes open and a knowing smirk clear on his lips.

"Mornin'," he drawls out slowly.

"Good morning," I smile back. "Thank you again…for last night."

"I already told you, there's no need to thank me. I'm here when you need me. I'm not going anywhere," he replies.

"I know, and I get that now. But I can still tell you how much it means to me," I tell him as I pick this moment to take my chance. I lift to my elbow and lean forward, letting my lips touch his for the first time in months. His mouth moves with mine, but I can feel his hesitation, unsure about what I'm doing. I pull back and his eyes are wide.

"What…uh…" his words are incoherent and jumbled, so I cut him off.

"Don't overthink it. Neither one of us can deny that there's still something between us, so why fight it. Let's just take it slow and see what happens. I thought a little thank you kiss would be a good test run," I grin at his gaping expression as I slip from the bed and move towards the bathroom.

After hitting up the drive-thru at Dunkin's, Kane pulls the truck into a tight parking space. I turn my head, wondering why we aren't heading straight for the highway. He clears his throat and my stomach drops. Something about the air between us has changed and this feels heavier than I'm ready to deal with.

"Before we get back on the road, there's something I have to show you," he says reaching into his pocket. He hands me a small paper napkin, folded into a tight square and I feel my eyebrows pinch in question.

"It's from her, your mother. She gave it to me last night after you walked out. It's her phone number. She said you can call anytime," his words wash over me as I grip the small paper in my fingers.

I pull the corner and open the napkin, seeing a phone number scrawled in blue ink. I quickly fold it again and slip it into my pocket. All these years, she knew where we were and she never once picked up a phone. I'll keep the number, but there is no way in hell that I will ever call that woman.

"We can go now," I tell him simply. His large hand reaches to touch my thigh and I lift to find his concerned expression.

"Are you sure?" he asks. I give a small nod in response.

"I am," I confirm and he shifts into reverse.

Chapter Twenty-Six

Kane

After another almost full day of driving down the highway, I'm fucking exhausted. It's only a few more hours to Rock Hill, but I just don't think I can handle another three hours of driving.

"I'm really fucking beat; do you mind if we stop for the night? We'll only have a few hours left to go in the morning," I run my thoughts by Ayla.

"I don't mind at all. I feel guilty that you've been doing all the driving," her response is sweet and the sound of her voice gets me stirring.

"I actually don't mind the driving, especially since I just got my license and my truck back," I share.

"That's right. I almost forgot," she replies innocently.

"Yeah, it was embarrassing as shit having Billy drive me around everywhere. Plus, I had to spend all hours at the garage. Normally I would use the tow truck to escape, but that wasn't happening. It was all oil changes and shit work," I tell her. "But at least this baby got fixed up and back to her original form," I lift my hand and let it slide smoothly over the dash.

"Sounds rough, but maybe you learned a lesson," she glances at me sideways, biting her lip and I just shake my head. She's sexy as fucking hell, and we both know she's right. I learned a hard fucking lesson.

"Are you hungry?" I ask. We stopped pretty recently to use the bathroom and we grabbed a couple drinks and small snacks, but I need to make sure she comfortable and happy.

"I'm good," she flashes me a smile and my dick jerks. Ever since that kiss this morning, my body has been on high alert and every little thing she does or says seems to set me off. Sharing a room again tonight might be rough on my manhood. Last night was bad enough. I felt like a fucking teenager again, having to sneak into the bathroom to rub one out after feeling her round ass pressed against me. I laid awake for hours while she slept, just thinking about all the things I wanted to do to her and the ways I wanted to touch her body. Jerking off in the bathroom seemed like the only solution at the time.

After pulling off the highway, it doesn't take long to find a hotel. I find a parking spot and kill the engine. She follows my lead, as we both climb from the truck and grab our bags to head inside.

"We need a double for one night," I tell the receptionist as I hand over my credit card before she can even ask. From the corner of my eye, I see Ayla do a small double take when I request the double room.

Shit. Maybe she doesn't want to take it as slow as I thought. I feel myself grin when I think back on it, knowing that slow has never been our pace.

Suddenly I'm fully aware that the girl behind the desk is giving me the once over. She offers me a wide smile as her eyes rake over my cut, focusing in on my Vice President patch.

"We have an excellent restaurant and bar on site, if you're interested," she suggests.

"Thanks, but we've been traveling all day. I think we'll probably stick to our room," I answer trying to make it clear that Ayla and I are together, despite my request for two beds.

"Well, if you change your mind, I'll be there after my shift ends," she tries. Ayla clears her throat behind me and I see the girl shrink, but only slightly.

"He said we'll be just fine in our room, but thanks for the suggestion," Ayla snips and I can't stop the low chuckle from leaving my lips. She's fucking claiming me and it's sexy as hell. She slips her hand into mine and I happily let her start to pull me towards the elevator.

"So, what was that all about?" I smirk as the elevator doors close and we're alone.

"I don't know," she answers, letting go of my hand. "I guess I just didn't like the way she was so obviously flirting with you." I take a step closer and hear her breathing change, but before I can do what I want, the doors open again cooling the air between us.

"You know you didn't have to get two beds. After last night, I think we're okay sharing a bed," her eyebrow lifts as we step into our room for the night. It's almost identical to the room we had last night.

"No, sweetheart. One night of being pressed up against you is about all I can handle. If you want me to take it slow, I think separate beds might be safer for both of us tonight," I grin back.

"Oh…" she breathes out as her skin flushes a soft pink.

I drop my bag beside the bed closest to the door and stretch my arms up over my head. My muscles are aching from sitting in the truck all day. I watch Ayla's hips sway as she moves around the foot of the bed, dropping her bag on the opposite side. Her jeans cling perfectly to her sweet round ass. God damn, maybe we should go down to the bar for a drink. I don't know how long I can keep my hands to myself if we stay alone together all night in this room, but I want to respect her boundaries.

"How about we go down and grab a bite and a drink?" I suggest.

Forty-five minutes later we're back downstairs sitting at a booth in the bar area of the hotel restaurant. They're definitely going for the sports bar theme, but it's a little over the top. They have sports photos and gear mounted on almost every wall, and multiple TVs lit up with different games. I lift my bottle of Bud and tip it back, taking a long drink as the waitress returns to slide a large plate of nachos in the center of the table.

Unfortunately, our change in venue is doing little to hold back my steadily growing lust. Every time she takes a breath my eyes move back to her spilling cleavage and the persistent hardness in my jeans has started to ache something serious.

"I'm going to run to the ladies' room. Could you get me another one of these if the waitress comes back?" she asks tapping the rim of her glass with her glittery fingernail.

"Sure," I reply easily. She turns and moves across the room, and I can't help but enjoy the view of her walking away. I lift my beer again; I'm going to need another drink too. And I have a strong feeling that I'll probably be spending a little more time alone in the bathroom tonight.

Just seconds after she disappears around the corner, the receptionist from earlier walks in, her arm locked with another female. She spots me right away and flashes a bright smile, quickly releasing her friend and heading in my direction. Shit.

"I see you decided to check it out," she approaches, walking right up to the edge of the table.

"Uh…yeah. Thanks for the suggestion," I reply trying to figure out the best way to handle this.

"Maybe I can buy you a beer," she smiles noticing the bottle clenched in my hand.

"No. I mean, thanks for the offer, but I'm here with my girl," I answer making it perfectly clear that I'm not interested in whatever she has in mind.

"Really?" she pushes and I feel the blood drain from my face when I see Ayla from the corner of my eye. God dammit. Why? Just when I think I'm making progress I get handed this shit.

Chapter Twenty-Seven

Ayla

I step around the corner, heading back towards our booth and my stomach sinks. The girl from the front desk is standing beside Kane, her hand on her hip as her fingers twirl in her hair.

"C'mon just one beer," I hear her begging as I approach the table. Kane's face is dark and somewhat unreadable, and a wave of nausea hits me as I wonder if maybe I interrupted something. Her eyes swing to me as I take my seat again, and she pushes out a little huff.

"Excuse me, am I bothering you?" I snap, unable to hold back my annoyance.

Kane's lips break into a smile and a deep chuckle vibrates from his chest. But I'm annoyed with him too. Why didn't he tell her to leave? It feels like this is always going to be a barrier between us. I want so badly to let him back in, but how am I supposed to trust him around other women. I turn away from her and focus on him, feeling my eyebrows pinch together.

"You think this is funny?" the anger begins to heat my skin. His posture quickly stiffens realizing that I'm not finding the humor in this situation.

"That's fucking rude," the nameless girl says under her breath just loud enough for me to hear and I'm done. I'm fucking livid and I'm not holding back any more.

"Rude? You want to talk about fucking rude?? Let's see…how would you feel if some random pathetic little whore was blatantly hitting on your man right in front of you?" I ream into her. Her eyes widen but she stays quiet so I keep going. "In case you were curious, I'm talking about you. Here's a tip for future reference, if a man is with another woman, leave him the fuck alone," I seethe.

She and Kane are both staring at me completely speechless. I direct my attention back to Kane. "Can I have the room key? I think I've had about all I can take tonight," I reach my hand across the table waiting for him to pull it from his pocket. He places the plastic key card in my palm, and I'm up and standing before he can object.

"I'll be right behind you. I'm just gonna take care of the check," he finally speaks.

"Whatever. Don't do me any favors," I spin on my heel and move away from the table as fast as I can without breaking into an all-out sprint.

Alone in the hotel room I finally feel like I can breathe again. I slip my booties off my feet and start to unzip my jeans, but just as I start to push them off my hips, there's a tap on the door. Kane gave me the key; he can't get back in the room unless I let him in.

I open the door and he steps inside, his large frame easily filling the small space. His eyes are dark and it's a look I've seen before. A pulse shoots deep through my core and the excitement settles between my thighs as he pushes the door closed.

His head drops and his lips cover mine without a single word being spoken. I let my mouth move softly against his. I feel myself caving, giving in to the feeling that's been building inside me since he showed up at Dad's house two nights ago.

Kane's thick arms wrap around me as he lifts me easily, carrying me towards the bed. His excitement presses into my center as I move my legs, lifting and wrapping them around him. The sensation is more than I can handle and I let out a moan, flooding his mouth with the soft sound. I'm still clinging to him as he carefully lowers us both and I feel the soft bed give under our weight. His lips leave mine and as he pulls away his dark eyes pull me in.

"I love you," he breathes out heavily and the sound of those three small words leaving his lips have me crumbling. "I need you to know you're the only one. The only one I want…the only one I'll ever want from now until forever," his words fall to my ears and I bite my lip to stop the trembling as small tears prick my eyes. I lift my hand to hold his check, feeling the scruff against my palm.

"I love you, too," I admit.

"I'm so sorry I hurt you…I…" he starts, but I touch a finger to his lips.

"I know," I breathe out and he leans forward, claiming my lips again.

My entire body pulses as his tongue curls with mine. He pulls back again, this time dropping his lips to my neck and my body quivers at the contact as he begins to kiss a soft trail down over my heated skin.

"God damn. You have no idea how much I missed you," his hushed words slip over my skin as he continues to kiss me in all the right places. My hands move over his biceps, feeling his thick muscle tighten under the soft cotton of his t-shirt before moving over his shoulders and raking my nails down over the supple leather hugging his back.

"I missed you more," I whisper.

"Not fucking possible," he lifts, flashing me a broad smile and I'm done for. I push my hands up under the leather, and then the t-shirt, needing to feel more of him. He lifts away from me, easily pulling both the t-shirt and leather cut away from his body in one quick motion. My eyes rake over his bare torso, lingering on the dark ink that's spread over his chest and biceps.

"Keep looking at me like that and we might never leave this bed," his voice wakes me from my daze and I lift my eyes to his face, finding a smirk on his lips and a dark desire flashing in his eyes.

His hands slip under my top and I know he's looking for the same gratification. I lift to sit, allowing him to peel the fabric away from my body. He pulls a sharp breath through his teeth and I feel my already heated skin flush under his gaze.

"Damn, sweetheart, you are a fucking vision. My memory didn't do you justice," his voice is rough and raspy with need. His words echo my own thoughts as my eyes continue to rake over the hard, sculpted muscles of his chest.

He lifts off the bed completely and I feel my eyes get even wider as he strips away his jeans. His dark boxer briefs cling to him tightly, giving me a clear image of his hardness waiting beneath the fabric. I start to push at my own jeans, already unzipped, but I can't seem to get them to budge.

"Let me help," he offers smoothly as he slides the denim down off my legs easily. He drops them to the floor with a soft thud before moving back to his own situation. In a second, his boxer briefs are gone and the only thing left between us is the thin lace fabric of my bra and panties.

He moves forward, letting his fingers brush my center before curling them under the edge to strip the soft lace away from my body. I tremble at the small touch. Even through the fabric, he creates a sense of pleasure I can't fully describe. My own fingers move to the front clasp of my bra, easily pulling the clasp apart and letting it fall away from my body. I am bare before him and completely vulnerable.

But I knew. I knew, long before he appeared on my doorstep, that Kane Donovan is all I'll ever want.

Chapter Twenty-Eight

Kane

Ayla is bare and beautiful and the sight of her spread and waiting for me takes my breath away. I could admire her body for hours and never get enough, but right now I need to feel her. I need to take her as mine again.

I make one more move, reaching down to the floor to pull a small box of hopeful condoms out of my bag. I tossed them in there about the same time I threw in the bottle of Jack. This trip could've gone either way and I needed to have my bases covered. I take one from the box before setting the rest down on the bedside table. I know once won't be enough, I'm keeping these little fuckers handy.

My fingers graze her ankle as I move between her legs, letting my hand trail higher until I can feel her pulsing heat. I use my teeth to tear into the wrapper and her eyes go wide as I roll it down to cover my hardened length. She shivers as I make contact, rubbing lightly against her waiting wetness. It's not going to take long for either of us this first time, but I've been dreaming about this for months and I intend to enjoy every fucking second.

Her hands grip my shoulders as I push into her. I watch her eyes roll back before finally closing, as her tight slit draws me in deep. Oh my fucking God. The way her body fits together with mine is pure fucking perfection. I pull back, filling her again as my own eyes close, my head tipping back and lifting towards the ceiling. Her pussy clenches and I feel her squeezing every fucking inch of me. I continue to move, the pleasure building with each slow thrust. My eyes drop back to watch her body as I try to take my time, but the vision of her is too much and I feel the burn deep in my belly.

"Look at me, sweetheart," my ragged request falls out and her eyes open to meet mine.

"Ahhh…" she breathes out and I feel her clench tightly around my cock. Watching her come apart under me is my undoing and I let a low groan vibrate from my chest as I find my own release. My hand lifts to touch her cheek and I bring my lips to cover hers, all while still buried deep inside her sweet warmth.

I pull back, lowering my body to lay beside her, my chest still heaving. She quietly rolls to her side and I can't help but wonder if she's second guessing her decision to let me have her again so quickly. I know she said she wanted to take it slow, but when it comes to her, I just can't help myself. My hand moves over her smooth skin, now sticky with sweat. I slide up and over the curve of her hips, stopping to rest my hand on her stomach as I touch my lips to her neck.

A feeling I can't explain washes over me and tightens in my chest. My gut twists as my fingers spread over her flat stomach. Only months ago, our baby was growing deep inside her. A vision of my hand on her big stretched belly fills my head. I clear my throat and push out a deep breath, knowing that I have to do this now.

"Can I ask you something?" I approach carefully.

"Well, this doesn't sound good, but go ahead," she replies quietly.

"Can you…I mean, after losing the baby, can you still have kids?" I ask as gently as possible. Her body stiffens against me and I hear her breath catch. Not the question she was expecting.

"I can," she offers a simple answer. I know I wasn't there for her during the loss and I should have been.

"It's just, I remember what you told me about your mom," I explain and my words start to spill out. "I'm sorry, I'll stop…we don't have to talk about this right now." She rolls to face me and her hand touches my chest.

"It's okay. We never really talked about it," she acknowledges. "Honestly I wasn't sure if you really wanted to know," her words sting a little, but I understand why she might think that, so I offer a small nod. "What happened with my mom was different. It was a lot more serious. They really only kept me at the hospital because I was dehydrated, it had nothing to do with the miscarriage," she explains.

"So, you can still…" I start.

"Yes," she cuts me off. "They did some tests at the hospital, and then I saw my doctor when I got back home. They think it had something to do with the IUD removal procedure, because all the results came back normal. They told me it was a risk, but it was weighing one risk against another, so I went with the doctor's advice. But I've had some time to process everything and honestly, I'm a little relieved. I'm sure that probably sounds horrible, but I'm not ready to be a mom right now. In a few years, maybe, but not right now," her honesty shocks me.

"Sweetheart, I will never forgive myself for not being there to take care of you," I reply with some honesty of my own.

"I know, but it's time to let that go and stop looking back. We can't change what happened, but we can be here for each other now," she leans forward pressing her lips to mine and I let my arms curve around her back, gripping her ass and pulling her close. A familiar feeling stirs below my waist and I need to feel her again.

"So, were you planning to use that whole box tonight?" she flashes me a bright smile as her hand drops and her fingers curl around my growing excitement.

"Is that a challenge?" I question as my lips curl into a smile and she breaks into full blown laughter. This girl owns me and if she wants, I will gladly use every single condom in that box tonight. I drop my lips to kiss the soft curve of her neck before moving to her ear. "Let's give it a try," I lower my voice and she trembles against me. This is going to be a good fucking night.

Chapter Twenty-Nine

Ayla

As we turn onto the street heading towards Ryder and Cora's, the cab of the truck gets quiet. Just as Kane and I reconnect with each other, we're getting separated again. We talked it over and decided to keep our reconciliation a secret for now. I love Cora, but I don't want to give her the satisfaction that her little plan worked. We'll tell everyone on New Year's Eve, at the party, but that means two days apart.

"You'll call me later?" Kane's rough question hangs between us.

"Yes, I'll call you later. I love you," I lean over and place a kiss to his cheek as he drives.

"I love you too, baby," he replies, his hand rubbing softly against my thigh. My body responds instantly and I contemplate asking him to stop and take care of me right here and now, but true to his word, we went through an entire box of condoms between last night and this morning. I close my eyes and inhale deeply, trying to force the feeling to pass quickly. My eyes open again, and he's pulling into the driveway.

The front door opens and Cora is a rushing blur coming towards me as I step out of the truck and close the door behind me. I look back through the window at Kane and offer a small wave as he starts to back up. Cora slams into me full force and my bag slips from my grasp hitting the pavement as her arms squeeze me.

"I can't believe you're finally here. I missed you so much," her excited voice fills my ear and I feel my own smile growing. She pulls back and her smile fades as she watches the truck pull away. "I guess the ride together didn't go over well?" she questions.

"I wouldn't really say that. We talked a lot," I tell her without giving anything away.

"But he's leaving. If it had gone well there's no way he'd be leaving," she observes, having absolutely no idea just how wrong she is. "C'mon, let's go inside," she says pulling on my arm. I reach down and pick my bag up off the ground and follow her lead into the house.

"Where's Ryder?" I ask after we've been inside for a couple minutes and he hasn't made an appearance.

"He's over at the clubhouse. They're having a meeting this afternoon, so he headed over there about twenty minutes ago," she explains. "The New Year's Eve party is going to be amazing. Oh, shit. Did you bring any party clothes, or should we plan a little shopping trip?" she asks with a new light shining in her eyes.

"I only brought jeans and t-shirts," I share.

"Then we definitely need to go shopping. You need something short and sexy to wear," she grins at me like only Cora can. "You can toss your bag in the guest room, it's all set up for you," she tells me and I start to move towards the room I stayed in during my last visit.

"I kind of thought maybe you'd be staying at Kane's," her voice follows me.

"Yeah, sorry to spoil your and Ryder's little set up. Kane showing up at my dad's house the day after Christmas was definitely a surprise. Especially since I was expecting a plane ticket," I call back.

After dropping my bag quickly on the guest bed, I walk back into the living room. I find Cora sitting on the couch, her face is slightly pale and her fingers twist in her lap.

"I'm really sorry," her voice is barely a whisper and a small wave of guilt hits me for keeping the secret, but I'm still not ready to tell her.

"It's okay," I sit down beside her. "Like I said, we finally got a chance to talk about everything and it was good, for both of us," I tell her. I've really missed her, and I can't let her feel too guilty.

"Really? You're sure you aren't like super pissed at me?" she asks.

"No. I know you were just trying to help, Cora style," I offer with a laugh and she smiles. "But it's not all on you anyway. Kane told me he had to talk you into the idea. Plus, he offered to buy me a plane ticket if I didn't want to ride with him, so ultimately it was my decision," I tell her.

"God, I really fucking missed you," she breathes out. I can't wait to see how she reacts when I tell her I'm staying.

"So, you said short and sexy. What are you planning to wear to this party?" I question and her eyes flash.

"Oh, I have a few ideas, but since we're going shopping, I'll look around a little more," she says and I can't help but giggle.

Almost four hours later we're pulling back into the driveway. A shopping trip, complete with a dressing room fashion show, was the perfect way to spend an afternoon with my bestie. I already knew that I missed her, but spending the day with her made me realize just how much. Watching her twirl around the dressing room, and hearing her laugh was the absolute best feeling.

Our arms are full of bags as we make our way into the house, finding Ryder relaxing in the living room. A broad smile fills his face.

"Hey, baby," Cora returns his smile. She moves towards him, leaning over to offer him a kiss. "What's got you so happy?" she asks.

"It's just not every day a guy like me has two beautiful ladies coming through the door," he chuckles and she swats his arm lightly.

"Welcome home, Ayla," he grins in my direction.

"Hi, Ryder. Thanks," I reply.

"I saw Kane this afternoon. You left my boy out in the cold, huh?" his eyebrows lift in question.

"Is that what he told you?" I ask, wondering what Kane really said to him.

"Actually, he didn't say much," he reveals. "But he told me he was heading to the gym when he left the clubhouse, so I figured he needed to work through some shit."

"The gym?" I question.

"Yeah, he didn't tell you?" he asks and I shake my head still feeling confused. "He used to hit the gym pretty hard, but between work and club shit, he let it go. He picked it up again during his thirty days away, and he's been lifting almost every day since he got out. I think it helps him stay focused or some shit," Ryder shares.

I had no idea. Kane has never mentioned the gym or anything about weight lifting. Despite being completely in love with him, we definitely still have a lot to learn about each other.

"Looks like you two did a little shopping today," he gestures towards all our bags.

"We got some really cute stuff to wear to the party," Cora bounces around the room.

"Do you want to show me what you got? I'd love a private show," Ryder's voice drops and I already know where this is headed.

"Not this time," Cora flashes a bright smile in his direction, and I see his eyes go wide.

"Fuck, baby. You know I can't take it when you tease me like that," he lifts easily from the couch and his arms move around her, causing her to giggle uncontrollably.

I back slowly out of the room, leaving them alone in the moment. They don't need me as an audience. I drop my bags on the bed and sit on the edge, pulling my phone from my pocket. I see a new message from Dad, he must've gotten my message when he got out of work.

**Thanks for letting me know you made it. Love you. Tell Cora I said hi.*

My phone beeps in my hand as a new message appears, this one from Kane. **Three nights with you and now I have to spend two alone. I'm fucking dying here.*

I can't help but laugh softly as I read it, but I actually know exactly how he feels. After spending the past three nights with him, tonight and tomorrow are going to be rough. It won't stop me from having a little fun with him though, as I type back, **I think you'll make it.*

It beeps again, **I'm not so sure…phone sex might help.* 😉

Oh my God. Really? I should have known this would be his response. I let my fingers move over the screen, fueling the fire.

**Cora and I went shopping today. I got two dresses for the NYE party. I think you'll like them.*

**Are you enjoying torturing me?* It beeps again in my hand.

I type back, **Just a little…*

Another notification hits my ear and I read, **did you tell her?*

I reply with a simple, **no.* And just as I hit send, Cora's voice carries into my room.

"Ay, we're trying to figure out what to do for dinner. Any ideas?" she calls.

"Let me think," I holler back as I type another quick message to Kane.

**Cora needs me. I'll text you again later. Love you. Xo*

I stand from the bed and slip my phone back into my pocket as I make my way back into the living room. I can do this. It's only two nights, I remind myself.

Chapter Thirty

Kane

It's only two nights, I remind myself for the twentieth time in about ten minutes. I can handle two nights. Working out for an hour at the gym helped, but a couple flirty texts and I'm on edge again. I'm fucking kidding myself thinking that this is going to be easy.

There's no way I can sit here all night alone, I'll drive myself crazy. I grab my sunglasses off the counter and head outside, throwing my leg up over my bike and starting her up. The vibration hums through me, offering the sense of calm I need. If I can't have Ayla, a ride on my bike will have to offer the release I need. The cool breeze hits my bare arms, tingling as goosebumps form on my skin. I feel alive on a whole other level when I ride. There is truly nothing else like the freedom I feel when I'm on my bike.

I finally come to a stop in Leia's driveway. I know my sister isn't expecting me, but I need a distraction, and this is probably the safest place to get that right now.

"Uncle Kane…Uncle Kane…" the boys run out, having heard me pull in. My sister has twin boys, Maverick and Mason. I always joke around and call them M&M for short. They're five and it gets them laughing every time. My sister definitely has her hands full. I'm sure they're gonna be hellraisers when they hit their teens. I remember the shit Fifty and I used to pull, and I just know she's in for some serious shit.

"Hey, M&M," I grin and they laugh. "Where's Mom?" I ask.

"She's inside making dinner and playing with Izzy," Mav answers quickly. Izzy is short for Isabelle, and she's my sister's youngest, and probably her last.

"Why didn't you come see us on Christmas?" Mason asks as we walk into the house together.

"I had to take a little trip, buddy. Did you get the presents I left with Mom and Dad?" I ask and both boys nod excitedly. I'm sure they're going to want to show me all their new toys and shit. They're the only grandchildren on both sides, so they get spoiled beyond belief.

"There's my girl," I smile down at Izzy when I step into the kitchen, finding her sitting on the floor stacking blocks.

"K…K…" she gives me a big drooly grin as she points at me. My sister closes the fridge and spins around.

"Well, welcome home. You know you could've at least called and let me or Mom know that you made it home alive," she chastises me.

"Sorry. I was a little distracted. Plus, I just got back in town this morning," I explain.

"So, where is she?" she asks trying to look around me, like I'm hiding Ayla behind my back.

"She's not here," I shrug.

"What do you mean, not here?" she tips her head in question.

"She's here, in town, but she's with her friend Cora. You know, the one Ryder's engaged to," I remind her. "She's staying with them for a couple nights."

"But you actually convinced her to come back with you; that has to be a good sign, right?" she asks and I can't stop the smile from breaking on my lips. I have to tell someone.

"It's so fucking good. Leia, she's gonna stay," I tell her.

"No way!" she rushes at me with open arms. "Mom is going to flip. Her baby boy is finally settling down. God, I can't wait to meet her," her words fall out in a rush of delight.

"What's all the excitement about?" Leia's husband, Jeff, walks into the kitchen. "Hey, Kane. You want a beer?" he questions pulling the fridge door open.

"Sounds good," I answer and he turns, handing me a cold can of Bud.

"So, what's up?" he asks again and I realize neither Leia or I ever answered his initial question.

"I was just telling Leia that my girl, Ayla, she decided to move here from New Hampshire," I say, and the words still seem unreal coming out of my mouth. She's really going to move here to be with me.

"Holy shit. I can't wait to meet the girl who finally managed to wrangle you in," he grins.

"Took him long enough," Leia chirps as she turns towards the stove, stirring something in a large pot.

"We don't all find the right one in high school," I chuckle.

"I guess not everyone gets as lucky as us," Leia's eyes sparkle as she leans in and kisses Jeff on the cheek.

"What's for dinner?" I break up the touchy-feely moment.

"American chop suey. Are you staying?" she asks.

"As long as you don't mind," I answer, lowering my heavy body to the floor and sitting beside my smiling niece. I start to stack the blocks up for her, but she reaches out and knocks them down, giggling uncontrollably.

"I think I know one little girl who's going to be jealous when Ayla finally makes an appearance around here," Leia's eyebrows lift.

"Not my little Iz," I grin, scooping her up and giving her a kiss on the cheek before setting her back down. "You're gonna love Ayla, just like I do. Aren't you?" I ask softly poking her belly and she flashes a big toothy smile giving me another adorable giggle.

I feel lighter already. Just sharing the news with my sister has me feeling like I can make it through these two nights, no fucking problem; knowing that Ayla is here to stay and I've actually said it out loud makes all the difference.

Chapter Thirty-One

Ayla

From my seat on the couch, I hear the door close and heavy footsteps move through the kitchen. My heart jumps to my throat. Kane didn't mention stopping by this morning, but I can't help but hope that he's here to surprise me.

"Mornin', Cora. Is the boss man awake yet?" I hear Fifty's unmistakable voice. I let the breath I was holding seep from my lungs as the disappointment fills my chest.

"He's in the shower, but we have some company in the living room. You might want to stick your head in there and say hi," she pushes and he rounds the corner, his massive frame filling the space.

"No fucking way. Ayla! Shit, darlin', you are a sight for sore fucking eyes," he grins and I stand to greet him.

"Thanks, Fifty. You always know how to welcome a girl," I smile back and he opens his arms for me to step into.

"Does Kane know you're here?" his concerned whisper fills my ear as his arms close around me.

"Actually, he does," I offer a simple response.

"Really?" he questions, cocking an eyebrow as he pulls back to look at my face. "Well, darlin', I gotta say, you look fucking fantastic," he offers a big smile without prodding any further.

"Hey, Fifty. Do you want a cup of coffee?" Cora calls from the kitchen.

"No, thanks," he answers while keeping his eyes locked on me. "Let's go get some breakfast. My treat," he offers.

"I don't know…" I mutter.

"C'mon. Please don't make me beg," he says and I feel a smile start to pull at my lips. "Go get some shoes on and meet me outside," he grins, knowing he's got me. I turn and as I step into the guest room, I hear Cora's hushed voice as she tries and fails at whispering.

"Go ahead and take Ryder's Jeep. It's probably not a good idea to put her on your bike. And don't keep her out too long. She's only planning to stay for a week, and I want as much time as I can get with her before she leaves. Plus, I really want to show her the Crystal Ballroom, it's one of the places I'm checking out for the wedding venue," I can't help but laugh to myself listening to Cora bossing him around. She's a tiny little thing, but she's definitely in charge.

"Don't worry, Mom. I won't traumatize her and I'll make sure I don't keep her out too late," Fifty chuckles deeply.

"Asshole," she laughs in response as the door clicks closed.

I slide my feet easily into my flip flops and skip back into the kitchen. Cora is leaning back against the counter, sipping her coffee. A small crooked smile forms on her lips.

"What?" I ask, knowing that look means something.

"Just be careful. You know I love you, and Fifty is the best, but he's also Kane's oldest friend. Kane will completely lose his shit if he thinks there's something going on between the two of you," she tips her head and I can tell that she's completely serious. Jesus, she's going to want to kill me when she finds out Kane and I are actually together and I've been holding out on her. I just have to hope that she'll be so happy when she finds out I'm staying in South Carolina, that she'll forgive me for keeping the secret and letting her suffer slightly.

"Oh my God, are you joking? Fifty is like a big brother, you know that and so does Kane. Even if he happened to find out, he would know that it's not like that. Stop worrying about me so much and try to enjoy a little alone time with your man," I smile and tip my head towards the sound of the shower still running. Her eyes light up as the words leave my lips and I know mentally she's already in the next room with Ryder.

As I climb into the Jeep, my eyes linger on Fifty's bike, left sitting in the driveway. It's a Harley, but the style and color look similar to Kane's bike. There's a strange comfort about being on the back of his bike, holding onto him tightly as we ride. I miss that feeling and I can't help but wonder if Kane feels the same way.

"I thought we'd just go around the corner and get some coffee…and maybe some pancakes, or whatever you want," Fifty's voice breaks into my daydream of the wind in my hair and my arms clinging to Kane as we ride.

"Yeah, that sounds good," I manage to answer. "What is it with you boys and pancakes?" I ask with a grin.

"They're just so fuckin' delicious. How can you not want pancakes?" he laughs lightly.

I hear the unmistakable sound of bikes approaching as we drive. My chest tightens with anticipation, wondering if it's going to be Kane. I catch the smallest glimpse as they pass, and even though it's only a second, I easily determine that it's not him.

"Looks like Sharky-boy and Billy are headed to pay the Pres. a visit too," Fifty observes. My mind instantly flashes to Cora. She's going to be disappointed that her alone time with Ryder is getting interrupted. Although I have a feeling that she won't have a problem putting either of those boys in their place.

Fifty and I are sitting snuggly together in a small booth at the little breakfast place he picked. It has a cute and classic diner feel, but it's definitely small inside. I couldn't help but smile as I watched him try squeeze his broad frame into his seat.

"Are you about done?" he asks as I continue to giggle at the image still fresh in my mind.

I nod and stifle my laughter, just as the waitress steps up to the side of the table. We're glancing over the plastic menus we found on the table, and as I look up to meet her eye, I see that she's already holding a pot of coffee in her hand.

"Good morning. Y'all want coffee?" she questions softly, lifting the pot.

"I'll take some," Fifty replies with a smile as he holds up one of the mugs already set in front of us on the table. I feel my eyes roll as I watch him checking out the waitress. Fifty can never seem to focus when there's a pretty girl around.

"Yes, please," I say holding my mug up too and she fills it quickly. "Thank you," I offer setting it back to the table and reaching for the small bowl of creamer cups.

"Do y'all need another minute with the menu?" she asks.

"I'm ready if you are," Fifty glances back in my direction and I nod.

"You go first," I say as I try to finalize my decision between French toast and eggs benedict.

After placing our orders, she turns to walk away and his eyes follow her. I feel a small giggle bubble up from my chest, and I try to stop it with my hand over my mouth, but he hears it.

"What?" he glares, already knowing what I'm thinking.

"You're totally checking her out. You make it so obvious," I laugh watching his eyes roll. "Maybe you should ask her out. She's pretty cute," I add.

"No way in hell. I don't date, remember," he offers the rough response I've heard from these guys more than once.

"Yeah…yeah. You guys are all talk," I laugh.

"Oh, really? I see how it's gonna be. I bring you out for breakfast and you wanna talk shit. If that's the case, let's talk about your *situation*, honey," he grins.

"There's nothing to talk about," I try to brush him off, but I can tell from the focus now on his face that he's not going to let me off the hook.

"Don't feed me that line of bullshit, girl. I saw the way you looked at me when I asked if Kane knew you were in town," he cocks an eyebrow waiting for me to give him something, but I don't and he keeps going. "You know he still beats himself up every day for what he did. I tried to convince him months ago to wake the fuck up and come after you, but you know what a stubborn S.O.B. he can be when he wants," he pushes and I feel my breath catch in my throat.

"What?" he asks raising his eyebrow again, knowing he's got me.

"It's nothing. I…I can't," I start to stutter.

"The hell with that. Spill it," he demands.

"Okay…" I hesitate, pulling in a deep breath and filling my lungs. "Well, what if I told you he did come after me. He is stubborn, so it took him a while, but he came. And maybe he knows I'm here because I came back with him," I reveal the secret, instantly feeling my skin heat.

"No fucking way! How? When?" his questions start to flow and I clear my throat.

"He showed up at my dad's place the day after Christmas. Only Cora and Ryder knew what he was doing," I share.

"So…*are you two*?" he questions and I understand completely, even though he didn't really ask anything.

"Yes," my voice is barely a whisper. "But no one knows yet, so you have to keep your mouth shut. No gossiping with the guys," my eyes narrow in on him. "Seriously, we want to surprise everyone at the New

Year's Eve party. Not even Cora knows, so keep it to yourself."

"Don't worry, darlin'. These lips are fuckin' sealed," he promises as he pulls the fake zipper across his lips and twists the imaginary key, tossing it over his shoulder.

Fifty and I continue to talk, catching up as we devour our breakfast. We laugh together, talking about Cora and Ryder's upcoming wedding and how the planning is already getting to her. I've been afraid of Cora's potential to turn into bridezilla, and based on what Fifty is telling me, it sounds like it's already happening.

"You're going to have your hands full trying to help her," he chuckles.

"Easy peasy. She's like my sister, I can handle whatever she throws at me," I smile hoping it's true. I slide from me seat and stand. "I just need to use the ladies' room, then we can go back to the house before she hunts us down," I joke, hearing him laugh as I walk towards the sign pointing towards the restrooms.

After quickly using the facilities, I step out of the stall and up to the sink. The door opens and our waitress steps inside, offering me an easy smile. As I turn the sink off and reach for the paper towels, her voice breaks behind me, echoing in the quiet room.

"Uh…so, this is probably going to sound a little strange, but I was wondering, are you with that guy? I mean, like really with him?" she asks and her face flushes a soft pink.

"No," I laugh lightly. "He's just a really good friend."

"It's just, I've seen him in here a few times recently, but he's usually alone," she offers as her fingers twist together.

"He's definitely single. But he runs with a bit of a rough crowd sometimes. They…uh… Well, to put it simply, they don't always keep their company for very long, if you get what I mean," I cringe slightly just thinking about it.

"Yeah, I definitely know that type," she smiles. "So, how did you end up as friends?" she questions and from the wide eyes she's giving me, I can tell she didn't mean for it to slip out.

"It's okay," I assure her. "I actually fell for his best friend," I shrug. As I stand here in the ladies' room with this girl, a lightbulb flashes brightly in my brain. "You know, we're actually having a big party on New Year's Eve. Do you know where Dawson's garage is?" I question and she nods. "Right across the parking lot, there's a clubhouse and bar. You should come, and if anyone questions you, just say I invited you. Oh, shit…my name's Ayla, by the way," I tell her.

"I'm Jade," she smiles back. "That actually sounds like it might be fun, as long as you're sure no one will mind?" she asks.

"Believe me, no one is going to object to you being there," I say and she flushes again.

"Thank you. I'll think about it," she turns and disappears into one of the empty stalls. I push the door and leave the bathroom, moving through the small dining area back towards the table. Fifty stands when he sees me reappear.

"You ready?" his deep voice questions.

"Uh huh," I nod unable to stop the smile from curling on my lips.

"What now?" he asks shaking his head.

"Oh nothing. I just ran into that cute waitress in the bathroom and she was asking about you and your situation," I tell him and his eyes go wide. "C'mon, let's go," I laugh, walking around him and heading towards the door.

Chapter Thirty-Two

Kane

The last two nights were bearable, but if I had to go another night, I think I'd fucking crack. Jesus, I can't wait to see Ayla tonight. I park my bike outside the clubhouse and move inside like I own the fucking place, although it's been a while since I came here to party. Regular club meeting and events, and shit like that haven't been a problem, but I've kept my distance during the normal weekend festivities. But tonight, is different. It's New Year's Eve and I finally have Ayla back here with me, and that has me feeling like the luckiest fucking son of a bitch on the planet.

The place is fucking buzzing when I walk in. I know Ayla is somewhere in the crowd, probably attached to Cora. I head towards the bar to get a better handle on the layout and my game plan.

"Hey, motherfucker. Is our V.P. actually gracing us with his presence? Where the fuck have you been hiding out every weekend?" Army's slurred voice hits me along with his hot breath.

"Fuck you," I let out with a deep chuckle. "It's New Year's, I wasn't missing this one."

"What can I get you, V.P.?" Timmy questions from behind the bar.

"Jack and Coke, double the Jack," I grin. "And pour one for yourself too, kid. It's New Year's and I'm in a good fuckin' mood. Let's have some fun tonight," I offer as he slides the glass in front of me. I lift it and touch it to my lips, letting the smooth drink run down my throat. "Shit, that's good," I breathe out.

"So, have you really been spending all your time at the gym?" Army asks.

"You fuckin' know it. I gotta be ready to kick ass at the drop of a hat," I smirk and he laughs.

"Any hot chicks there?" Fifty asks as he sidles up beside me. Leave it to him, he's always got the ladies on his mind.

"Fuckin' A. Of course, there are, and I bet they're all wearing tight-ass pants and bending over and shit," Army says, practically drooling.

"Jesus Christ. You two need to get fucking laid," I laugh.

"Well, shit, brother. That's the plan tonight. I just need to narrow down the field. There are some fine ass honeys in this place tonight," Army chuckles.

"Damn right. I got my eye on a curvy little thing over by the pool tables. That long brown hair, shit…take a look, brother," Fifty's eyebrows raise and I turn my head, looking over my shoulder.

Motherfucker. Time to play along.

"No fucking way," I breathe out the words, feigning surprise at seeing her.

"Yup," Fifty's voice drops down beside my ear, a little too close for comfort. "I had breakfast with her yesterday," he grins but I can't take my eyes off her.

She's sitting comfortably on one of the soft couches beside Cora. I watch her tip back a small shot glass and they both laugh; Ayla's cheeks flush a warm pink. My girl is a fucking goddess, and I want to march right over and show everyone that she's mine, but I know she has a plan and I have to try to play this cool. She stands from the couch, and even across the room I can pick her voice out from the crowd.

"No, I'll go get more. I'll be fine," her sweet voice flows right to my ears.

"You knew she was here?" I question, finally turning back to face Fifty.

"Yeah, but so did you," he grins as if he knows. I offer a simple shrug, not even trying to deny it.

"She told you, didn't she? Shit, you two are like fucking sisters," I shake my head, laughing loudly.

My eyes move back to Ayla, watching as she weaves through the crowd. Her short, gold dress sparkles as her hips sway. She looks happy and my chest swells just watching her and knowing she's mine. She steps up beside our small group at the bar, only a couple feet away from me. Her arms lay flat on the bar, as she leans over, her ample cleavage popping out from the low-cut neckline of her dress. There's no way I can pretend when she's this close. I'm going in.

"Ayla, what can I get for you?" Timmy asks with a bright smile. A little too fucking bright.

"Cora and I need a few more shots. Four of Cuervo and then two cans of the fruit punch Truly," she tells him before turning and flashing me a smile. She's well aware that I'm checking her out, and she knows just what she's doing to me.

"Hey, Timmy. Put your eyes back in your fucking head," I growl. Watching him eyeball her tits as she bounces lightly to the music while he pours her drinks, is some shit I won't let slide. Her eyes are slightly glazed when she swings her attention in my direction. If she drinks much more, she's going to be fuckin' trashed.

"I can take care of myself," she smiles. "And, I wore this dress for a reason. Sometimes it's nice to be looked at," she motions towards the cleavage spilling from the gold fabric clinging perfectly to her curves. I raise my hands in surrender.

"Fine, sweetheart. I'll let Timmy eye-fuck you all night if that's what you really want," I smirk back despite the fact that my fists are now clenched tightly at my sides.

"I didn't say that's what I want, I just said you don't get to stick your nose in," she blinks her long lashes at me and I can't stop myself from leaning in close.

"It's not my nose that I want to stick in, sweetheart," I whisper and her body stiffens. I pull back catching her wide-eyed look and the soft pink flush glowing over her skin, and I take a second to enjoy the response she's giving me.

"Fuck, Kane, she's in a feisty mood tonight. Good luck, brother," Fifty grins as he moves away from the bar. He stops beside Ayla, whispering something in her ear before making his way across the room. Army turns, following behind him without another word.

I slide down the bar, until I'm standing right behind her. I can feel the heat coming off her skin as I lean into her and pull in a deep breath, filling my nose with her sweet scent. She lets out a soft breath and I can see she's fighting it.

"How much longer do we have to play this game, sweetheart? I missed you," I admit.

"I…" she hesitates trying to regain her composure. Her ass rubs against the front of my jeans, just enough to raise my dick to full attention. I hear her breath catch and I know she can feel it as I press into her. I touch her hair, moving it to one side, giving me access to the soft skin of her neck. My lips drop, placing a quick kiss to the surface, and her body trembles.

"You almost ready to let me help with that ache?" I smile against her ear and she pulls in a long deep breath, giving me exactly the reaction I wanted and I press into her deeper.

"Yes…" the word is a whisper on her breath, but I hear it loud and fucking clear.

"Come with me," I grip her hips and turn her body, guiding her towards a door hidden behind the bar. Timmy raises an eyebrow.

"I will be locking this door," I tell him and he nods. He's smart enough not to question me. I follow closely behind her as we step through the door and into the darkness of the small room. I pull it closed and flip the lock. We're finally alone.

"Everyone's going to know now. No more keeping it a secret," her voice is soft as she steps closer to me and her lips brush against my neck.

I flip the light switch and a dim lightbulb glows above us, revealing the small storage area. My hands move to grip her hips, lifting her easily and setting her down on the small counter space. I push at her dress, moving it up her hips. She lifts her ass slightly, and I grip her panties, quickly pulling them down and away from her body. My eyes drop to find her sweet pink center before lifting back to her face. Her eyes are wide and her body is humming for me.

"Lean back, sweetheart," I request. She pushes her ass to the edge and leans back as far as she can, resting her head against the wall. My fingers trail up her inner thigh before making contact. Her body bucks against my touch and I feel the smile spread across my lips. She's fucking primed and ready.

I slip two fingers into her waiting warmth, watching her reaction as I pump softly against her slick wet heat. Her fingers curl around the edge of the counter as she lifts into me, her body begging for more.

"You like that, baby," I drop my lips to her ear as my hand continues to work between her thighs.

"Yes, Kane…more…" she begs.

This room is too small, but I need to get a fucking taste. I lower my body and enjoy the sight of her body as she accepts my fingers sliding into her over and over. I move forward, letting my tongue move over her soft pink folds. The taste of her sweet juices dipping on my tongue as I continue to lick her pussy turns me into a wild man.

One of her hands breaks free from the counter and her fingers move through my hair, gently holding me in place. I feel my lips curl into a smile, knowing that she fucking likes it as much as I do. She's actually holding me here and damn if I don't want to make her come all night long.

"Oh…God…Kane…yes…" her words are short and breathy, and full of need. She's almost there and I want to push her right past the breaking point. I pull back for just a second, watching my fingers continue to work.

"Come for me, sweetheart," I beg and I feel her instantly clench at my request. I dive back in, feeling her melt on my tongue as I turn ravenous.

"Ahhh…" she moans as her legs shake and I enjoy the fruits of my labor. She's so fucking sweet. As soon as her body relaxes, I stand and my hands move quickly to my belt. I see her eyes drop to the front of my jeans, there's no hiding my excitement straining at the fabric.

"Here?" she tips her head in question.

"I need to be inside you, now," I growl as I pull the zipper and slide my jeans down off my hips, holding my thick cock in my hands. "You want this, don't you?" I ask and her body gives a visible shiver. She definitely wants me to fuck her. Her hand moves forward, encircling my rigid shaft and I let out a ragged breath at her touch.

"Fuck, sweetheart. Two days without you was way too fucking long," I groan. She presses me against her hot dripping entrance and her big blue eyes look up at me through her lashes.

"I need you now," she begs and I can't fucking breathe. I slide forward, filling her warmth and molding our bodies together. She shifts her hips and I slowly rock to meet her.

"God damn. Your pussy is like fucking heaven," my words pour out as my hands slide under her ass, lifting her easily and thrusting deep inside her tightness.

I need Ayla more than I've ever needed anything in my entire life. She's my air, my sustenance, my fucking everything. I can't survive without her. I need her to know just how much she means to me. Her legs tighten around me, pulling me deeper and her eyes lift to meet mine.

"I'm yours. I'll aways be yours," her whisper kisses my neck and I feel her deep muscles clench around me.

"Fuuuck…" a deep roar tears from my chest as my release hits full force and I spill into her. Her hands lift and lock around the back of my neck, pulling me down to touch her lips. She lifts to sitting and rests her head softly against my chest as my arms wrap around her, holding her against me.

"I love you, sweetheart. I fucking missed you so much," I tell her and I'm not just talking about the last two days, I'm talking about the last five months and all the time we lost. She pulls back from my chest and I know she feels the weight of my words as her hand moves to my cheek.

"I know, Kane. I know. I needed time, but I'm here now and I'm not going anywhere. I love you," her words wash over me in a wave of raw emotion and I feel my chest tighten.

"So, do you think anyone saw us come in here?" her question rings in my ear.

"Oh, shit, yeah. You know how nosey those sons of bitches are. I guaran-damn-tee that at least one of them was watching us, and now they all fucking know. But, if you want to try to be discreet, I'll let you go out first," I offer helping her down from the counter so she can fix her dress.

"No. It's been too long already. I don't want to pretend anymore. Let's just go out there and let them all see that we're together," she smiles and I feel my cock twitch again.

"Are you sure you want to go back out there? We could just stay in here for the rest of the night," I smirk.

Chapter Thirty-Three

Ayla

After pulling my dress down, I search the floor for my panties. Grabbing them, I slip them around my ankles and drag them back up my legs. Standing, I look around and can't stop the small giggle that bubbles out as I take in our situation.

"What?" his deep voice questions.

"I can't believe we just did that in this tiny closet with a room full of our friends right outside," I acknowledge. "Maybe I shouldn't drink any more tonight," I offer him a smile, sure that the shots Cora and I were doing had a little something to do with my lapse in judgement. His thick arms move behind my back as he pulls me tight to his body and I feel my skin heat again.

"Sweetheart, believe me when I say that I will take a taste of you anytime and anywhere I can get it," he flashes a broad grin. I feel my mouth drop and my knees feel weak as a pulse runs deep through my center and I'm ready for him to take me again.

"We…we should get back out to the party," I manage to push the words past my lips, despite what my body is saying. I take one more glance down at my dress, smoothing the shimmering sequin fabric down over my hips, and adjusting my neckline so I'm not completely exposed. When I look back to Kane, I find his eyes dark and his jaw clenched tightly.

"What is it?" I question.

"God dammit. I just got you back and I'm already fucking this all up," his voice is softer than his expression, but I'm still completely confused.

"What are you talking about? How could you possibly?" I start to question, but he cuts me off.

"After everything, I didn't fucking learn. I touch you and I have no fucking self-control what so ever," he says, but it's almost like he's talking out loud to himself.

"Kane, I don't understand," I say touching his arm.

"I just fucked you bare. I didn't use a condom. After everything you went through, I'm sorry," his head drops. I loop my arms around his heated torso, feeling the muscles hidden beneath the layers of fabric clinging to his body. Lifting to my toes, I place a soft kiss to his lips.

"I'm okay, and I'm on a new birth control, so please don't beat yourself up for making one mistake. I'm on the pill now, so we should be okay…at least this one time. We'll use condoms from now on. It's not like you planned this," I offer him a small smile and he nods his head, but I can tell he's still letting the guilt hang on.

"As long as you're really okay," he finally breathes out and I nod.

"C'mon. Let's go get a drink and enjoy New Year's Eve with our friends. This is our fresh start," I tell him and his eyes move to my face, shining with unspoken hope.

He finally turns and opens the door, stepping out in front of me. He turns back and offers me his hand, and I join him back in the large room. My eyes rake quickly over the crowd, trying to determine if anyone is watching or waiting for us to reappear. I see Timmy raise an eyebrow in our direction, from behind the bar, and Kane catches it too.

"Prospect, if you even dare to fucking speak of this, I will come for you," he threatens and I see Timmy shrink slightly.

"I don't have any idea what you're talking about V.P.," he responds.

"Good boy," Kane praises his answer. "Now, can you pour us a couple drinks?"

With our drinks in our hands, I follow as Kane leads me towards a small group of our friends. We find Ryder and Cora curled together on a small couch, and I'm surprised to see Fifty appearing deep in conversation with Jade, the waitress. I smile at her and offer a small wave as we approach.

Cora's eyes are wide when she sees me and Kane join the group together, and I offer her a small nod. Her face lights up, and I know I'll eventually have to answer for keeping it a secret, but right now she's happy for us. Kane drops to settle into one of the large leather chairs, and his hand taps lightly against his knee.

"Come sit with me, sweetheart," his deep voice drawls and I drop into his lap without argument. This is where I belong.

"Well, holy shit. It's about God damn time," Mickey steps up from behind, gripping Kane's shoulder. His laughter flowing through our small circle of friends. Kane lifts his glass, a broad smile filling his face from ear to ear.

"Here's to the best fuckin' New Year's Eve I've ever had. Cheers, boys," he offers and they all raise their glasses.

Six months later...

Chapter Thirty-Four

Kane

I lean back against the door frame, watching Ayla on the couch with Izzy curled up in her lap. Every time I see her with Leia's kids it just confirms in my mind that she'll be an amazing mom one day. She looks up at me and offers a soft smile as she reads a book that she's already read three times. Izzy wants to hear it again, and of course, Ayla won't say no.

"Kane, she is just the sweetest thing," Mom sneaks up behind me and whispers at my side as I tip back my beer and take a long drink. No matter how much time Mom spends with her, I hear this every time. She absolutely loves her, just like I knew she would.

"I know, Ma. She's about as close to fucking perfect as they come," I reply, still unable to look away from the view on the couch.

"You better hang on to her, because I love her too," Leia chimes in from behind us, still cleaning up in the kitchen.

"Oh, I intend to," I tell them both. My wheels have been fucking spinning for weeks, trying to figure out the best way to make it happen. As much as I would've liked to ask her months ago, she still needed time. I had to let her adjust to living here, and make sure it was really what she wanted. And while I'm not normally one to get approval before I do anything, I had to in this case. I had to talk to the other man in her life. And thankfully, despite being a cop, he actually fucking likes me.

Like a fucking whirlwind, the twins burst into the room, chasing each other. I let Mom and Leia deal with the scene, as I make my way across the room towards my two favorite girls.

"K…K…" Izzy points excitedly.

"Hi, sweet girl," I drop down and kiss her forehead softly before turning and finding Ayla's full lips and taking them without remorse.

"Ewww…" Mason whines seeing us kiss and I pull back, standing tall again.

"You can think that now, little man," I grin at my sister and shrug.

"You almost ready to hit the road, sweetheart?" I ask Ayla and her wide eyes look up at me. My cock jerks against my zipper and I push out a deep breath. The things she does to me with a simple look, even with my family filling the room around us. There's no doubt about it, I'm fucking hooked. I clear my throat.

"I…uh…I just figured Leia might want to get these kiddos in bed soon, and I have a feeling they're not going to settle down until we leave," I explain and she nods.

"We're going to head out too," Mom announces behind me, obviously eavesdropping on everything I've just said to Ayla.

"Come over here and give your mother a hug, especially since you're leaving next week," she says and I turn. Her arms move around me, hugging me tightly. "Have fun next week, but stay out of trouble," she whispers a warning against my ear, like only a mom truly can, and I can't stop the smile from curling on my lips.

"Goodnight, Ayla. Enjoy your visit with your dad," she says over my shoulder.

"Thank you," Ayla returns brightly. Her excitement has been building for weeks and now that we're heading back to Laconia on Thursday, she's just fucking beaming. She can't wait to visit with her dad.

"Night, Dad," I call over Mom's shoulder and into the kitchen.

"See ya," he grumbles back and I know he's probably already half way out the door. I'm sure he was ready to go as soon as we finished eating. Mom gives me one more quick squeeze.

"Guess I better follow, before he leaves me here and I have to sleep on your sister's couch," she jokes turning and disappearing into the kitchen. "I love you," she calls over her shoulder.

"Love you too, Ma," I say before turning my attention back to Ayla and nodding my head towards the door, casually questioning again if she's ready to leave. She stands with the little one who's now dozing in her arms. Leia sneaks up and I watch as they carefully make the swap with Izzy.

"Bedtime, baby girl," Leia whispers.

"We're gonna get out of your hair," I lower my voice, trying not to wake Izzy. "Thanks again for dinner."

"Anytime. Have fun in New Hampshire, and make sure you text or call so I know you're safe," she adds.

"Don't worry, I'll text you," Ayla smiles as my sister turns, carrying her sleeping daughter to bed.

Ayla's arms hug me tightly as we ride home. Being on my bike with my girl on the back is the best feeling, well, a close second to having her in my bed. The warm air flows over me as I drop my hand and drag my fingers up over the smooth skin of her bare leg. In just a few days we'll be on our way to another bike week in Laconia. It's hard to believe it's been a year since Ayla walked into my life, or more accurately, since I rode into hers. I have a feeling that this year's trip might change me even more than the last one.

Chapter Thirty-Five

Ayla

My arm stretches across the bed, finding Kane's side empty. He's been having trouble sleeping for the past few weeks, but he doesn't want me to worry, so he waits until I fall asleep and then he sneaks out to the garage to tinker with his bike. I pull back the blanket and slip from the bed, moving quietly through the house.

Peeking out the kitchen window, I see the glowing light spilling from the garage. I wish he would just tell me what's on his mind, but some walls have been harder to break through than others. It's been almost a year, and I can't help but wonder why he still won't let me in completely.

I'm so excited that we're heading to bike week in Laconia in a few days. I can't wait to see Dad. I felt really guilty leaving him at first, but then Wendy moved in to the house, and it makes me feel so much better knowing that he's not alone.

I open the side door, and slip out into the cool night air, letting my bare feet guide me through the damp grass. I push the garage door open and find Kane leaning over one of his toolboxes. His body stiffens slightly before turning to meet my gaze.

I chew on my bottom lip as my eyes linger on his sweaty torso, his damp t-shirt clinging tightly to the thick muscle I know is hidden beneath. He pulls a sharp breath through his teeth, and his darkened eyes rake down over my body in return.

"God damn, sweetheart. Don't get me wrong, because you look fine as hell, but did you really just walk across the yard in your panties?" his deep voice questions.

"It's three a.m. I'm pretty sure no one noticed," I grin.

"Come here," he requests and my body hums at the thought. I step forward and lift my hand to touch the scruff covering his cheek.

"Please tell me what's keeping you up. Maybe I can help," I plead, but he shakes me off. He's not going to give me any answers tonight. He already has other things on his mind, as his hands move around me, sliding down over my lower back until his large palms cup my bottom.

"This is all the help I need," he whispers against my hair and I feel the familiar pulse deep between my thighs.

"Take me back to bed and I'll be more than happy to help," I smile up at him.

"No need to go anywhere. I think you can help me out right here," he smirks and I feel a fresh wave of heat spread down over my chest.

My hands drop to the front of his jeans and I hear his breath catch as I make contact. I lift to my toes, placing a quick kiss to his lips before slowly lowering to my knees. My fingers move quickly at his belt and zipper, freeing his rigid cock. My eyes widen and my mouth waters as I drink in the sight of him. I move forward letting my lips curl around his massive length as my tongue tastes the saltiness clinging to his smooth skin.

"Fuuuck…" he groans deeply as he leans in and his fingers twist into my hair. I let my hand slide over him, slowly working his hardened length as I continue to pull him deeper into my mouth. "God damn, baby," he breathes as he brushes the back of my throat. His legs tense and the sweet warmth floods my mouth, coating my tongue and running down the back of my throat as a rough growl tears from his chest.

His hand moves from my hair, as he helps me back to my feet as I swallow what's left. The relaxed look now filling his face gives me hope that he'll come back to bed with me and get some much-needed sleep.

"Damn, sweetheart. I honestly don't know what I ever did to deserve you," he grins and I can't help but smile back as I lift and touch my lips to his cheek.

"Are you ready to get some sleep now?" my question is a whisper.

"Not even close," he smirks before dropping his lips to my ear. "Panties off and bend over the bike," he requests.

"Wh…what?" I stumble over the simple question.

"You heard me. I want you on my bike," he practically growls and I feel the flood rush between my legs.

I shimmy out of my panties, sliding them off my hips. He reaches out, taking them from me and looping them around the handlebars, the thin lace fabric swaying. His hand touches my cheek and his lips cover mine, pulling all the breath from my lungs.

He pulls back and his dark eyes are wild with need. His large hands grip my hips, turning me until I'm facing his bike. His hand moves smoothly down my back, gently pressing me down until I'm resting flat against the leather seat. He continues to slide down over the smooth curve of my ass cheeks before moving between my thighs. He gently pushes my legs apart, widening my stance before letting his fingers find my waiting wetness.

"Ahhh…" I breathe out when he finally makes contact. My body pushes back against him, needing to feel more of him as he works my aching pussy. His warm body steps closer, moving in behind me and I feel his hard cock press against my bottom and my entire body quivers.

"You want it, don't you?" his husky voice asks, practically begging me to say it. He always gets off on this part.

"Yes," I answer through my now labored breathing, his fingers still moving over me. He pulls his hand back and I feel his hardness at my waiting entrance. He rubs against me, coating himself in my juices and my body bucks as he slides over me, making contact with my sensitive clit. Shifting forward, he fills me quickly and easily and I let out a soft moan at the fabulous pressure he creates in my belly.

His movements are slow and controlled, going deeper with each thrust, as he sinks into me over and over, his fingers digging into my soft skin as he holds my hips. My legs feel weak and begin to shake as the exhaustion hits my body and I approach the edge. My muscles clench, tightening around his hardened length and my body trembles as I finally let go. The feeling he creates within me as our bodies move together is pure ecstasy.

"That's it, baby. Yes…fuuuck…yeeesss," he groans as he spills into me, filling me deeply.

He pulls back and I lift my tired body back to standing and he wraps his arms around me from behind, dropping his nose to my neck.

"I love you, sweetheart," his soft words kiss my ear as his lips touch my shoulder.

"And I love you," I offer in return.

I reach forward and slip my panties off the handlebars, then I spin around, still locked in his arms. His face and body are both clearly relaxed. And I realize that even though I still don't know what's keeping him awake, right now, it really doesn't matter. I gave him what he needed and I'll be here for him whenever he needs me. He'll tell me his secret when he's ready.

"C'mon. Let's go back to bed," I look up at him and he nods in agreement.

Chapter Thirty-Six

Ayla

"Dad, why did you make so much food? You're going to have leftovers for months," I laugh. I think he got so excited at the fact that Kane and I were coming for dinner our first night here, that he prepped way too much.

"Well, I figured your friends would be hungry after traveling," Dad answers and I feel my eyebrows lift in confusion. As if right on cue, the sound of bikes pulling up out front fills my ears. I turn to Kane, who tips back his beer, looking completely relaxed.

"You invited the guys?" I ask. He swallows and cocks a playful eyebrow.

"Of course. You know those boys need to eat too," he smirks and I suddenly get the feeling that he's up to something. Why would he invite all the guys to my dad's house and not mention it?

"Ayla, could you come inside and help me bring out the rest of the food?" Wendy asks and I nod.

"Of course," I answer. I lean down and drop a quick kiss to Kane's forehead. "I don't know what you're up to, but I will figure it out," I whisper before turning to follow Wendy's lead into the house.

"Good luck with that, sweetheart," he chirps as his large hand makes contact with my ass cheek and I glance back over my shoulder. His eyes are unreadable, hidden behind a pair of dark sunglasses, but the broad smile and deep chuckle vibrating from his chest give me a good indication of his mood, and I'm happy to see him so relaxed.

"Christ, I think your dad bought enough to feed an army," Wendy laughs as she starts to pull bowls from the fridge.

"Don't worry. These guys definitely know how to pack away the food," I tell her.

"Ay, are you in here?" Cora's voice questions through the door. I turn to find her peeking through the screen, her hand lifted and shading her eyes.

"Yeah, just come in. You can help us carry the rest of this food out," I say and she pulls the door open. "Is the whole club here?" I ask as she steps into the kitchen.

"Of course. You know these guys would never turn down free food. Although, I'm not sure this will get touched," she laughs picking up a large tray stacked with veggies.

"So, I think we're all planning to go over to High Octane later," she bumps my hip playfully. "Are you gonna come out tonight?"

"I don't know. We just got here, and I wanted to visit a little with my dad tonight," I tell her.

"But it's our first night here. Don't you want to go out and have a little fun," she whines. "It'll be so much better now that we don't have to work," she reminds me.

"I'll have to see what Kane wants to do," I say, but even as the words leave my lips, I can already pretty much guarantee that he's going to want to go out. I honestly think he's been needing this week away almost as much as I have. But while I've been excited to see my dad, Kane really just needs a week to relax and hopefully get some decent sleep.

"Of course, he'll want to go. Just give the boy a glass of Jack and sit on his lap and he'll be set for the night," Cora laughs and I feel heat rise in my cheeks.

"Cora, baby, what's taking so long?" Ryder's deep voice calls through the screen.

"Girl talk. We'll be out in just a minute," she hollers back and the shadow of his large frame moves away from the screen. "Why are the biggest boys always the neediest," she grins and I can't help but laugh. Her act doesn't fool me, I know she eats up every bit of attention Ryder gives her. She is absolutely glowing. She fucking loves it.

With our arms full of food, the three of us move back outside to the waiting group of hungry men. I set the dishes down on the surface of the table, and before I can turn, Kane's large body closes in around me.

"I missed you," he whispers against my hair.

"I was only gone for about five minutes. You look like you survived just fine," I smile.

"I like seeing that smile on your face. Are you happy to be home?" he keeps his voice low and I nod, leaning back slightly against his chest.

"Mmmhmm…" I breathe, fully enjoying the feeling of him pressed into me so closely. He is right though, I am happy. As much as I love living with him in South Carolina, I have really missed my dad. And it's really nice to be back here and see how happy he is with Wendy.

Kane's hand leaves my hip, and I feel his arm move between our bodies as he reaches into his cut.

"Are you still wondering why I haven't been sleeping?" his words are soft and I feel my eyes widen. Why is he bringing this up now?

"What?" my confusion is clear as the single word hangs in the air between us. And as I wait for him to answer, I realize the yard is quiet and everyone is watching us. His hand moves back in front of me and a small black velvet box sits flat in his palm.

"I wanted to surprise you. I've been planning this for weeks and I wanted it to go perfectly. Go ahead, open it," he tells me.

My breath is wedged tightly in my throat as I lift my hand and touch the soft velvet. I lift the lid slowly and the sun hits the teardrop shaped stone. It's a pale smokey gray, like nothing I've ever seen before. It's truly beautiful. I feel my lower lip tremble, and I'm glad he still has a grip on me, otherwise I think I'd be on the ground.

"It's some type of quartz, but I can't remember the name," he shares, but it's not important right now.

"What…what are you doing?" I manage a whisper.

"You're mine, remember?" he questions with a soft chuckle against my neck. "But more importantly, sweetheart, is that I'm yours. I have been since the first time I saw you; it just took me a little longer to admit it. But right now, in front of your dad and all my brothers, I will gladly say it. So, do you think you might want to spend forever as my ol' lady?" he asks and I can feel the weight of the question as everyone watches.

"Yes…yes…of course, yes," I answer through a now steady stream of warm tears flowing over my cheeks. I turn in his arms, finally curling into his chest and he hugs me tightly. I pull back and he touches my cheek softly, wiping the tears away before dropping his lips to mine.

"Put the sucker on her, already!" Army calls across the yard, and I feel a smile curl on my lips as Kane pulls back. He draws the ring from the box and lifts my hand, sliding the ring down over my finger.

"Now show that off, sweetheart," he smiles from ear to ear and I lift my hand, showing all our friends the sparkling rock now secured tightly around my finger. The crowd erupts around us and Kane's head dips once more to cover my lips. My hands touch the back of his head, moving through his hair as I savor everything about this moment.

When we finally break, I look to my dad. His eyes shine with unshed tears and I don't think I've ever seen him smile so brightly. He moves towards me and I step into his open arms.

"Did you know?" I ask as he squeezes me.

"I did. Kane wanted to do it here so that I could see it and be a part of it. You know, just looking at the guy, I never would've thought he was good enough for my little girl. But he proved me wrong. He really does love you and seeing you happy like this, it's all I've ever wanted for you. I love you, Ayla," he whispers.

"I love you too, Dad," I tell him and he loosens his grip.

I watch Ryder step up and shake Kane's hand. "I told you you'd be next," his deep laugh fills the air around me, and I feel my eyebrows pinch in question. But before I can ask, Cora pounces.

"I can't believe it! Now we're both engaged!!" she squeals as her tiny arms wrap around me.

"Holy shit, brother. It took you fucking long enough," Fifty grins as he steps up and grips Kane's shoulder before turning in my direction. "Give me a hug, darlin'. Make it quick before Kane goes all caveman," he laughs loudly as he pulls me in for a strong hug. "I saw this coming a mile away. Congrats," he whispers in my ear and I feel the tears pooling again.

"Alright, alright…that's enough," Kane steps up and Fifty releases me easily, smirking.

"I fucking saw that coming too," he adds with a deep chuckle.

Kane's arms circle around me and I feel his warmth seep into my skin as he holds me to his chest. I pause, letting my eyes move over the scene now filling my dad's backyard. Leather clad MC members drinking beers and eating hamburgers and hot dogs. This is truly a sight I never could have predicted. But my dad is all smiles, and this group has without a doubt become my extended family. I love each and every one of them and I can't imagine my life without them.

Acknowledgement

I honestly cannot even believe that it's been almost two years since I started my writing journey. Writing and being an author is something that I never even imagined, and now I can't imagine my life without it. Some days I wish I had found it sooner, but I know that it came into my life at a time when I really needed it and for that I am so thankful.

I am also so incredibly grateful for the overwhelming support from my readers. You have welcomed me and embraced my stories and that is a feeling that I can't even describe. Thank you for reading and your kind words of encouragement and support.

As always, I also have to thank my family. My husband and two daughters who support me and my dreams on a daily basis. While my husband enjoys joking about the subject matter of my stories, his unconditional support always amazes me.

With so much love – *Thank you!*

About the Author

Samantha Montague is the author of the Attraction Series. She has always loved reading, especially fantasy and romance stories. In 2020, she was introduced to the Wattpad platform and discovered a new passion for writing.

Sam was born and raised in New England, where she still resides with her husband and two daughters.

Find her at samanthamontaguebooks.com, on Instagram @samanthamontague_author, and on TikTok @smontagueauthor.

Additional books from Samantha Montague

The Attraction Series

Mia leaves her comfortable life in California behind to start fresh in Boston. In a new city, at a new school, she makes quick friends and is drawn into the world of college hockey. Mia meets Dex and feels and instant and undeniable attraction. *Could it be love?*

Follow as Mia and Dex discover each other. In a whirlwind of romance, tears, and laughter, this is the love story you've been waiting for.

Made in the USA
Columbia, SC
23 August 2024

40951147R00133